# Shunned by the Pack

*Rejected Mate*

*Book Two*

Alexa B. James and Calinda B.

*For all my kinky peeps.*

# **Chapter One**

*Axel*

The crickets surrounding the woods and marsh near the vampire's lair make so much noise my head wants to explode. Or maybe my head wants to detonate because my mate stands before me. Luna, her hair a glorious shade of purple, is trapped in a cage like a dog, teeth bared like I'm the one who put her there.

I'm going to tear the vampires' limbs from their bodies with my bare teeth for this.

She must have been in her skin when the vamps took her, as now she stands there naked. It takes every ounce of willpower in me not to rip apart her cage and take her in my arms.

I don't think she'd like that very much, though.

The enormity of my mistake hits me again. I insisted on severing our mate bond, and now I wish to hell I

1

hadn't done something so drastic, even to protect the pack. And yet, even though the elder destroyed the bond, turning the crescent moon on my arm into just another battle scar from my life, I can't get Luna out of my mind. Thoughts of her haunt me like a banshee, wailing for the dead.

"Luna," I say, staring at her through the bars of the cage they put her in. I can smell the burns on my hands from the silver, but I can't let my wolf heal me right now. I have to stay in human form and convince her to come home.

"Get away from me," Luna snarls.

"Luna," I say again, the rest of the words I want to say clogged in my throat.

"Leave me alone."

"I can't do that, Luna," I say quietly. "You're in my bloodstream. You consume my every waking hour and haunt my dreams like a wraith every night."

I step closer to the cage again, but she backs away, looking over her shoulder. When she turns back to face me, a look of anguish torments her features, and the nights' shadows darken her expression. Without answering, she lifts her palms and studies them.

In the faint moonlight, I notice the blisters on her palms, and rage throbs in my temples. Those fucking vampires. She must have burned the shit out of her hands when she gripped the bars of the cage, too. I'd give anything to take her pain away right now.

"You're coming home with me tonight," I say firmly. "There's no other choice."

"Why should I?" she demands. "You *broke* me, Axel. You left me ruined."

She sniffles, and my chest tightens until I can barely breathe. "I'm sorry. You know how fucking sorry I am."

"You got no idea what it's been like for me since you dragged me out of the swamp," she says. "I didn't want to be bonded with you or anybody. I didn't know what it meant at all. And then to have that bond *erased*…" Her voice cracks, sending a million glass splinters through my heart.

"I know," I say miserably, because there's nothing else I can say. Every word from her lips is the truth.

She crosses her arms defiantly over her tits, fuller now than when we found her half-starved in the swamp. "And then I find out you demolished my home in Bogbeast Waters. You're nothing but a liar and a betrayer. I'm not going anywhere with you."

I swallow and continue. "I was wrong to sever the bond between us, Luna. I was trying to do my job, to look out for the pack's safety and put them first. I didn't think I had a choice."

She casts her gaze at the ground.

"I should have been more patient and taught you everything you need to know," I admit quietly. A man like me, an Alpha, doesn't admit he's wrong easily, but I can't stand the thought of her hating me so much. She deserves the truth. "I should have treasured you as the most precious thing in the world, because that's what you are. I'll do anything to get you back. Anything in the world. Name it, and it's yours."

A shrewd expression forms on her face. I can almost see the chit she's stored in some pocket in her mind, which she'll bring out and use against me at a later date. "Anything?" she asks.

I swallow again and nod. "You'll see—I've changed. Things will be good with us when I bring you home. I'll make sure of it."

"My home will *never* be with you," she says in a voice so low I shouldn't be able to hear it—but the intensity pouring through her words comes through as if shouted them into a megaphone.

Luna loathes me, pure and simple.

"I'm going to get you out of here," I promise. With a sigh, I pivot and stride along the damp ground toward the vampire's lair.

At the door, I lift my hand and hammer against the metal and wood. The sound seems to echo and dissipate, like swamp fog swirling around the trees.

"They're not there," Luna calls.

It's the first thing she's said to me in a civil tone since I arrived—I'll take it as progress.

"Then I'll find them," I tell her.

Vampires stink like ash and death, so they shouldn't be too difficult to track down. Just as I pivot to go on a blood-sucker hunt, a vehicle pulls into the driveway. It looks old and elegant, a 21st-century Bentley, and it gleams like polished silver in the faint moonlight.

Evan and Drake, two of the nastiest vampires in Jacksonville, emerge from the car, talking loudly and grinning like they've just scored crimson meals and hot pussy.

Evan rounds the bumper of his vehicle, still chatting with Drake. But then he stops, stares at me, and lets his eyes flash with red.

I return an equally assaulting glare. "I've come to get my woman."

"Have you now?" Evan's lips curve into a cold smile. "What makes you think we're going to give her up?"

"You don't like the taste of wolf, for one. She's young and inexperienced. She's of no use to your kind."

His smile becomes a taunting grin as he saunters toward me. *"You're* here, so I guess the bitch has a use after all."

I clench and unclench my fingers. "What do you want, blood-sucker?"

Evan stops and stands before me with Drake by his side. "You know the answer already. We want territory. Give us Creebay Preserve, and we might have a deal."

His request slugs me like a fist to the gut. Creebay Preserve is all the hunting ground the pack has left. Our pack fought for that land as Florida sank into the sea and every creature's habitat shrunk. Creebay is a tiny fraction of the land we once hunted, but it's all we could carve out for ourselves in the new world. The pack once commanded the hundreds of acres making up Bogbeast Waters, until the hurricanes and tornadoes claimed it as their own, making the swampland unfit to live. Only panthers and a few strange souls choose to live in Bogbeast, side by side with the swamp monsters, ogres, and alligators.

The two vampires move in on me, and though they have a few inches on me, I stand steady, unafraid. I could shift and rip their tonsils from their throats if I chose to. But killing them wouldn't get Luna back—one wolf can take out a few vamps, but not a whole army of them, and I know there are more on the way.

"Creebay's not an option," I say. "It's our hunting ground."

"Then Luna is not an option for you," Evan says with a shrug, pushing past me.

"Wait," I say, trying to calm my raging heartbeat.

"Why should I?" Evan says, standing before his front door. He shoves his hand in his pocket and retrieves a few jangling keys.

I glance over at Luna, standing stock-still in the middle of that fucking cage with her arms hanging by her side, and my heart tears apart. "We have some other property in South Jacksonville, closer to the ocean. We haven't done much with it because there's no game for hunting, but I'll consider giving you a piece of it. It's called Dead Waters. It would be perfect for your clan."

Evan barks out a laugh and turns to face me. "You're a funny one. Dead Waters is called that because it's dead. The land and all its occupants. Nothing can live there."

"You don't have a beating heart. Why should it matter?" I know I'm grasping at straws. Dead Waters is one of the foulest bogs on the planet, thanks to the disasters that left it uninhabitable.

"Let's see," Evan says, making a show of tapping his lip with his forefinger and directing his gaze skyward. "Do I want a piece of land where I'll have to wade through four feet of water to get to my home in the treetops? Or do I want the Creebay Preserve with its lush forests and waterways and the perfect spot for a domicile worthy of my stature? Hmmm. I can't decide."

I glance at Luna again. Wet streaks glisten on her cheeks.

A flare of pain shoots through my chest. The only way we managed to secure Creebay was to sign treaties granting hunting rights to a few of the other supernaturals as long as they stay out of our way. What will happen if I give our territories to the vamps?

I turn back to Evan and Drake, who both stare at me with eyes like cold gunmetal.

Then, the fatal blow to my heart occurs—Luna shifts into her wolf form, throws back her head, and howls in anguish.

Evan grins widely. "Oh, this is rich. She's got you by the short and curlies, Wolfie."

"Shut up," I snap. I work my lips between my teeth as I consider my options. "I can grant you ten acres in the north."

Evan laughs coldly. "Ten acres? That's hardly worth the toilet paper you wiped your ass with this morning."

He pivots and fits his key in the lock.

"Okay, thirty acres," I say as Luna continues to howl.

"One hundred, and you've got a deal," Evan says, twisting open the door.

The entire preserve is only two-hundred acres. How can I possibly give the vampires half of our territory? "Fifty," I counter.

"Seventy-five," Evan says, still keeping his back to me.

My teeth grind together. Luna's cries are like jagged metal twisting into my body. "Sixty," I say, as the earth crumbles beneath my feet.

"You have a deal," Evan says, tossing me the keys. "Unlock your bitch, and we'll sign an agreement."

As I rush for my mate, he calls after me. "We'll assume ownership at once."

I'm sure they will. I've got a shitload of explaining to do to my pack. But first, I have to convince Luna to come home, or I just gave away almost half our land for nothing.

# Chapter Two

*Luna*

Axel opens the door of the cage and steps inside, holding out a hand to me. I don't want to touch him, especially because both of us have shifted into our human skin, and being so near to him only reminds me of the last time we were together without clothes between us. I avert my eyes and shake my head.

"Luna, come on," he says. "I just bargained to set you free. You can't mean to stay here."

He's right, but I'm not happy about it. He sees my hesitation and steps back, giving me a good amount of space so I can step out of the cage without touching him.

"Good," he says when I'm out. "Now let's get to my truck before they capture us both."

Without warning, he scoops me up over his shoulder and takes off. I cling to his neck, afraid he'll drop me if I let go. I don't want to go home with him, but I'm not staying with the horrible monsters who stole me away from my loves, either. As soon as I'm able, I can escape to the only place I can truly call home.

I want to be with the triplets.

Axel sets me gently in the front seat, leaning around me to buckle the belt across my lap. His thick shoulder brushes my bare nipple, and it hardens against him. I suck in a breath, shocked by the ripple of pleasure his touch brings. I don't want it, though. His pleasure comes with too high a price.

Axel swallows and leans back slowly, his eyes searching mine. I turn my face away and cross my arms to hide my jutting nipples. He closes the door and starts around the truck. This is my chance. If he takes me back to his house, he might not let me leave, and I don't want to make Callan come get me again, not after the triplets told me that the pack wants them dead.

The second Axel turns the corner to the driver's side, I yank open the door handle and bolt into the swamp. My feet squish through the sodden ground as I race across the landscape. I will make it back to my men, make sure the vampires didn't hurt them.

I hear a curse and footsteps behind me. I run faster, my heart racing as he chases me through the swamp. I don't want to go anywhere with him. I want to be with Callan, Warrick, and Ethan—they're the wolves I consider my pack now. If they think I'm dead, it will break their hearts. I have to tell them I'm okay.

I hear Axel getting closer, and I put on a burst of speed, but I don't have time to stop and shift. The next second, Axel catches me from behind, his arm wrapping around me.

"Let me go," I scream as he hauls me off my feet.

When he sets me in the front seat of his truck again, he stands like a tree in the door, blocking my way out. "I can do this all fucking night," he says. "You can run, and I can catch you."

My nostrils flare as I regard him. He's right. I'm wholly famished and weak with hunger. I need food, water, and a long sleep after being unable to lie down in the cage.

But first, I've got to get back to my men.

I wait, breathing hard, as he backs around the front of his truck, keeping me pinned to the seat with his gaze. Once he's inside the cab, he fires up the engine and takes off.

That's when I make my move, flinging open the front door and pitching my body out. I fall onto the sand and dirt road, scraping my shoulder. I quickly shift and take off, limping slightly from my injured limb.

I hear Axel shout, and the truck skids to a stop, but I'm deep in the underbrush before he has a chance to exit the driver's side door.

The scent of the swamp lures me toward its watery oasis, so I put on more speed. I long to disappear into the misty wetlands, hide for a while, and find my way back to the triplets. Thoughts of them are the only thing that's keeping me going. A few minutes later, a large black wolf rockets through the marsh, sinks his fangs into the ruff of my neck and takes me to the ground with the force of his attack. With his teeth clenched tightly against my fur and flesh, he secures me to the damp earth with his forepaws.

15

I'm so weak my struggle must seem pathetic. I can feel his body on top of mine, and something exciting and confusing ripples through me. I'm not scared of him, even though he hurt me before. I know, somehow, that he won't hurt me again. That even though I'm pinned to the ground, I have some sort of power over him. I don't like the confusing sensations rolling through my body, so I snarl, snap, and writhe beneath his bulk, digging my claws and teeth into whatever I can get my paws on.

Axel shifts suddenly, still pressing me to the ground beneath his forearm.

I shift, too, and suddenly our hot skin is pressed together. We're both panting from the run and the struggle, and even though I hate him for what he did, I feel a stir of hunger in between my legs when I feel his cock pressed to my thigh. His length begins to stir and harden, and as I stare into his eyes, I feel my heat throbbing with desire. The energy between us shimmers like hot coals, waiting to erupt into flames.

Axel's tongue darts out and wets his lips, and my thighs clench at the memory of that tongue stroking my heat until I exploded. I want more. I don't think about anything, just spread my legs and shift my hips so he's between them. He sucks in a breath when his rigid cock meets my sensitive flesh. I gasp, too, rocking my hips against him in a desperate attempt to ease the ache growing inside me.

"Luna," he growls. "What are you doing?"

I rock my hips faster, grinding against him, wild with need. "Help me," I whimper.

"Oh fuck," he groans, pushing up on his hands and watching me wriggle and writhe and buck under him. "You're soaked. Did being chased turn you on?"

His words bring back the reason for this, and I give him a forceful shove. He doesn't budge. He's staring down at my open thighs, his cock against the wet heat between.

"Why is your pussy shaved?" he asks quietly.

"Get off," I yell. I shove him again, and this time, he willingly rolls from my body, though he's far too strong to be moved by the force of my little push. His swollen erection bobs between his legs, and I nearly buckle at the sight. I want him so bad it aches in my blood, my bones, my wolf. I never had these feelings before leaving the swamp, and I don't know how to keep them from controlling me.

Until recently, I lived alone with my mother in Bogbeast Waters, with no contact with anyone but her. I was naïve, and even though it was a constant struggle to care for Mama and her moods, I stayed content. As long as I brought home a good catch every day and could keep Mama from tearing down the house in one of her fits about being watched by wolf packs or murdered in the night, I could rest easy.

Now I'm all over the place, with mood swings like a 'coon swinging from the Spanish moss, flying from one tree to the next. I wonder if this is how Mama's moods felt from the inside, since I only saw them from the outside.

Tugging my mind back to my current situation with this maddening man across from me, I drag the back of my hand across my lips. Axel watches my every move, as hungry and wanting as I am. But I don't want to want him. I want to hate him. I leap to my feet and sprint away again, through the palmettos and pines. I hear his footsteps coming hard and fast behind me, and again, he catches me. He lifts me off my feet, growling into my ear.

My body explodes with shivers of heat. I writhe and kick, my foot connecting with his shin, and he takes us to the ground. He pins my hands, his body matching mine on all fours. I can feel his cock, and I arch my back, pressing back against it, panting for him to fill my throbbing core. My wetness coats my center, my thighs, his thick cock.

"Axel," I moan, grinding against the heat of his cock. It keeps slipping away when I try to push back onto it, impaling myself. "Help me."

In one motion, he flips me onto my back. I open my legs eagerly, and he sinks between them, his cock pushed firmly against my entrance. I wriggle and pant, trying to get him inside, where the need is gnawing at me maddeningly.

"And you'll behave?" he asks, his eyes boring into mine.

"Yes," I breathe, my fingers curling around his hands that hold mine to the ground.

He gives one powerful, slow push, sinking his cock into my slick channel, opening me and filling me with the delicious stretch I needed. I cry out, digging my nails into his hands, bucking my hips under his. He stays pushed up on his hands, watching me squirm, dig my heels into the ground, and beg for more. But he doesn't move.

"Axel, please," I beg. "Just… Just—"

I break off, finding the spot that feels so good when I grind it against his pelvic bone that I see stars.

"What?" he growls, his hands crushing mine into the ground, his hips holding me impaled.

"Fuck me," I whimper. "Please."

He grinds his pelvic bone slowly against me, and the angle his cock hits inside me pushes me over the edge. I shriek and arch up, my body gripped in some kind of muscle spasm, my sheath squeezing rhythmically around his cock, though it hasn't moved once. The explosion is so strong that for a second, all I see is black, with a billion stars strewn across my vision. My cries fill the swamp, making the insects and birds fall silent. Axel looms over me, watching me writhe and convulse under him.

At last, when I settle back into my body, back to the earth, he pulls his erection out of me, where it stands straight and glistening with my body's pleasure.

My need having been fulfilled, the hatred I feel for him settles back into place. He crouches before me as he wipes the blood away from his lip and hands. My teeth must have connected with him when he had his fangs sunk into my neck or had me pinned. Good. I hope he needs stitches. Better yet, I hope he bleeds out and dies.

I sit up, swiping angrily at the pine needles stuck to my elbows. A warm trickle of blood drips down my own neck from where he caught me in wolf form.

"Let me tend to your wound," he says, his eyes landing on the blood.

"Why should I?" I ask, shying away.

A little smirk tugs at the corner of his lips. "I'll make you come again."

"Come where?" I demand.

"Where you just did," he says.

I stare at him, conflicted silence filling the air between us. I want more of those feelings, but I don't want him near me. I like that he didn't get any satisfaction for himself, that he kept his body separated from mine and just watched me find the place where everything is perfect and blissful and nothing feels bad.

Axel crawls forward over me again. I say nothing, just sit on the ground as he licks my neck, collarbone, and the top of my left breast with his tender tongue. The feel of his tongue is intoxicating as it sweeps along my bare flesh. He cradles my body and lays me back on the ground, his mouth latching onto my nipple. Pleasure spikes through me, sharp and sudden, and I cry out. He slides his hand between my thighs, stroking through my slick folds and rubbing his thumb across the little bud that throbs every time his tongue pulls on my nipple.

His mouth moves across my chest, his lips tugging and nipping at my skin, his tongue lathing over my other nipple. I whimper helplessly, borne up and out of my body by the pleasure he keeps pouring into me. He slides two fingers into me as his lips close around my other nipple and suction to me. I bury my hands in his hair, gripping his head, pulling him in while he pulls me into his mouth, sucking my nipple until it aches from pleasure. His fingers pump into me relentlessly, his thumb caressing the swollen, tender bud in my pussy until I'm moaning and writhing.

He lifts his head, swiping his tongue up the column of my neck to my ear. "Come for me, Luna," he murmurs, his voice throaty and hot in my ear.

A shiver of pure, erotic longing goes through me, and my body is wracked with shudders of bliss as my hips rise, my walls clamping down around his fingers as I explode again.

When the last of the shudders in my body subsides, he sits back on his heel, licking my juices from his fingers and watching me with hooded eyes. His gaze is clouded with fevered longing, his cock still straining against his skin, standing up against his belly.

I'm too spent to move, to stop him if he tries to mate me again. I don't care. I feel so good, so relaxed, I think I'll fall asleep at any moment.

"Look," he says at last. "I know you're pissed. You have every right to be angry. But we can't leave you here in the woods alone. The vampires will only capture you again and do worse harm to you. Let me take you home. I'll make you feel good any time you want. If you hate it there, if you can't stop despising me, we'll make another arrangement. Okay?"

I file away his promise, the same way I filed away his assurance that he'd do anything to get me back while I stood in the vampire's horrible cage, and then I nod. Axel scoops me up in his arms and starts back toward the truck. Instead of fighting this time, I drape a lazy arm over his neck and let him carry me like I'm his catch of the day.

As we trek through the swampland, the sun punches its way over the horizon, clearing the way for the dawn.

Axel sets me gently in his truck and buckles the belt around me. He hesitates a second, then leans in and buries his nose in my lilac hair, taking a long, deep breath. I watch his cock bob against his belly before he pulls away.

When he climbs in his side of the truck, I relax against the door, but I'm already plotting my way back to my men. Axel can make my body feel good, but only they make my heart sing.

Axel drives us out of the marsh and into the chaos of Jacksonville, with the cars careening toward us at breakneck speed, making me nearly scream before they zoom past without touching the truck.

We power past derelict neighborhoods, fallen into disrepair. Stores and shops where humans and supernaturals purchased clothes and food stand in the middle of water where there was once dry land. Seas are rising as if the earth's liquid wants to flush away the civilization that has made such a mess of this sacred land.

At his house on Golden Glade Street, Axel parks the truck and strides around to my side to hold open the door for me. Silently, I slide from the leather seat and back into his arms, feeling safe and cared for despite what he's done in the past. He makes his way across the soggy ground of his yard, up the steps of his front porch, and into his small dwelling. Once more, thoughts of the triplets fill my heart with longing. Axel's house is cleaner and just as big, even though he lives here alone, but it's his home, not mine. What are my men doing? Are they looking for me, feeling as lost without me as I do without them?

But once we cross the threshold, I stiffen as I catch sight of Ama lounging on Axel's sofa.

"Ama, get up," Axel snaps, suddenly seeming angry, though I'm not sure why. "And for fuck's sake, put some clothes on."

A wounded expression crosses her face.

Axel sighs. "Look, I'm sorry I snapped, Ama. I've had a rough night. I had to… *fuck*." He sinks onto the couch, still cradling me in his arms. I give Ama a smug smile, enjoying the withering look she's giving me.

"So, she's back?" Ama asks, smoothing her thick, straight hair over her shoulder.

"For now," Axel says. "I had to do some fucked up shit to get her back, though."

Ama puts her hand on his back, arching a brow at me like she's waiting to see if I'll react. I want to tear her fingers off with my canines, though I'm not sure why I care that she's touching him.

Even Axel notices her attempt to draw him into her greedy spider web, and he scoots away from her and settles me onto the couch.

"I have to talk to the pack right away," Axel says. "I'll call a meeting. Make sure Luna feels welcome and gets settled while I'm busy."

He stands, then turns back and crouches in front of me. I notice his cock is finally hanging down, like it's given up and accepted defeat. "You can tell Ama anything you need," he says. "She's here to serve you while I'm gone."

"I think I need to eat something, and then I need sleep," I murmur. I can barely keep my eyes open.

Axel snaps his fingers in Ama's direction. "Get Luna some food."

Ama's mouth works around, settling into a sullen line before she rises. "Of course, boss. Right away."

Axel bristles. "Without the attitude, please. I'll get the bed ready for Luna before I go. She needs to rest."

He heads up the stairs toward his bedroom. After he's gone, Ama turns to me with a sneer. "He's fair game, you know."

"What?"

"He chose to break your True Mate bond because *he doesn't want you*. Can your dumb brain understand that?" She scrunches her face up in an ugly way.

"He went to a fair bit of trouble to get me back," I point out. "He must want me for something."

"You had your chance," Ama says in her snarly voice that grates against me like sand ground into sunburned skin. I feel her more powerful wolf looming over mine, and my wolf whines and begs to retreat from the threat. "Now stand down. He's *mine*."

I don't want to be with Axel, but the words spewing from her mouth make me want to fight her to the death—if only I had an ounce of fight left in me. "Aren't you supposed to be fixing me some food?" I ask.

"I'm not your servant," she snaps, glaring at me.

"But Axel is your Alpha, and he told you to serve me." I lay my head back against the sofa, drawn by the lure of sleep.

Ama's nostrils flare, and hatred burns in her eyes. "Axel feels sorry for you. You're nothing but a pathetic, uncouth little mutt who's brought nothing but trouble to our pack. The only reason he wants you here is because he hates those disgusting heathens you've shacked up with, and he doesn't want them to have you."

My heavy eyelids sink shut. "I didn't ask to come here."

She says nothing, but I can feel her scorching my skin with her eyes. "He'll never love you," she finally says. "He wanted to break the bond, and there's a reason for that. You're not a suitable mate for an Alpha."

"Uh-huh," I mumble, giving way to my body's demands.

"He's going to love me. Just you wait."

"Mm-hmm."

"He'll be mine, so you better watch yourself around him."

I let out a yawn. "Then why'd he give up half of your land to get me back? Answer me that?" I open my eyes long enough to witness the shocked expression on her face, like someone lit a bomb under her butt.

I feel Axel's presence a moment before he steps into the room. As he scoops me up, I give way to slumber before he even delivers me to bed. My last thoughts are that he'll have some explaining to do with Ama and the pack that apparently won't accept me, and I'm fine with that, because the sooner he gives up on keeping me, the sooner I can get back to the three brothers whom I adore.

# Chapter Three

*Luna*

I don't know how long I sleep, but when a hand touches my shoulder and shakes me, I rocket to consciousness, fists flying, ready for a fight.

"Easy, Luna," Axel says, ducking, palms up to fend off the blows. "It's just me."

"Just you," I say, blinking at the fading light outside. I must have slept all day. My chest feels as empty as my belly, aching for the triplets and not this man who betrayed me so badly.

"Ama prepared some food for us," Axel says. "I sent her away so we can have time to connect."

Groggy as hell, I scrub my face with my hands, trying to wipe the sludge from my brain. My bruised, confused heart clatters about in my chest. "We're never going to connect," I say, "but tell her thanks for the food next time you see her."

"I will," he says simply. "I'll get you some clothes."

I sit up and yawn again, stretching my arms over my head. The dust lining the side table catches my eye. I drag a finger through it, hold my finger before my lips, and blow on it. A tiny cloud of particles wisps into the air and slowly floats toward the floor.

When I'm done, Axel has brought me an oversized shirt and a pair of soft pants that must be his. His jaw looks like rigid glass as he glances away from me. "I've let things go a little since you've been gone."

I pull on the clothes even though they're six sizes too big. "You mean since you severed our bond and cast me from your pack."

The muscles in his jaw tighten and bulge. His skin pulses near his left eye, and I'll bet if I were any other wolf, he'd have flattened me by now for my insolence. My neck would be seized in his sharp teeth, and I'd be pinned against the floor. The thought makes me squirm a little, the way it did when he chased me through the woods.

"Let's eat," he says, stepping away from the bed.

We pad downstairs, ignoring the groans in the old wooden steps. Wrinkled gray curtains hang around the front window. The sofa is made of worn, cracked leather, the color of a raven's wings, while a low table made of shabby wood slats sits in front of it. A large, extended slab of wood affixed to the wall serves as a shelf. There's an old turntable resting on the shelf, right next to a globe. A smaller rack made of wire hangs above the turntable, filled with old vinyl records from the last century, kind of like the one the triplets have back home.

"Luna," Axel says, interrupting my inspection.

"Right," I say. "Food prepared by Ama, eating and connecting."

Axel takes my arm gently, and I allow him to guide me into his kitchen and help me into my seat—a simple chair made of the same wood slats as the table in front of the sofa.

Similar gray curtains line the small window in the kitchen, too. Wood shelves lined with stacks of mismatched plates, bowls, and sturdy drinking glasses sit on the wall above the countertop and stove. It's fancier than the triplets' kitchen for sure.

Axel moves around the kitchen with quiet confidence, pulling bowls and plates from the shelves and filling them with food that smells delicious, despite being prepared by a hateful woman.

When Axel sets a plate of meat and vegetables in front of me, my stomach cramps with hunger, and I dig into the food without another thought. Manners—something the triplets tried to teach me—are forgotten. I'm too hungry to consider them.

Axel settles into a seat across from me and patiently waits for me to finish. When I'm done, he reaches for the white cloth next to my place setting, shakes it, and hands it to me.

I grab it and wipe the gravy and juices from my face before licking my fingers.

Axel eyes me as I groom myself, saying nothing.

When I toss the napkin on the table, I lean back in my chair, lifting the front two legs from the table, the way Ethan would.

"I'm sorry you lost your mother," Axel says quietly. "The healer said she did all she could."

"I didn't *lose* her," I say, folding my arms across my chest the way Callan did. "She died."

Axel finishes chewing his bite of food, but he doesn't snap back at me. "I'm sorry you've endured so much tragedy in such a short time."

I grunt the kind of response Warrick did all the time when I lived with the triplets. I'm guessing that Axel's apologies are more sorries than he's ever uttered in his life, what with him being an Alpha and all. It kind of thrills me to witness how I've affected him. I feel that same power I felt in the swamp when he had me pinned, but I knew that somehow, I was the one in charge.

Axel takes another bite, watching me while he eats slowly and neatly. A thick, smothering silence hangs between us. The floorboards creak and settle from somewhere in the house.

"What do you want from me, Axel?" I ask, letting the front legs of the chair fall to the floor with a loud thunk. I stare at him in a manner I would never have been so bold to try when we met. It's a look that conveys how much I loathe him and how much I long to have him inside me, defiant but almost hoping he'll command my submission the way Warrick did.

"I want you to be my mate," Axel says simply, returning the smoldering gaze.

My betraying body's response is instant and intense, and I feel heat shimmering in the core of me, where he pushed his cock earlier and let me feel it buried there until I came apart. I swallow hard, squeezing my knees together. "What if I don't want that?"

Axel tips back his head and sniffs the air, then drums his fingers on the placemat in front of him. A smile plays at the corners of his mouth. "I think you do."

"I liked what you did today," I say, acknowledging the desire humming through my system. "So if we mate again, will that be enough, or do you want something more?"

"I want more," he says, his fingers crumpling the napkin next to his plate into a ball inside his fist. Then, he pins a lust-filled gaze on me and slides the tip of his tongue along his upper lip.

A thrill of excitement wiggles through me. I squirm in my seat and look away from Axel.

"Like what?" I ask, staring at my empty, blue-rimmed plate. I pick it up and lap at the juices lingering on the porcelain. When I set it back down on the table, Axel's still staring at me with hooded eyes. A simple look from him is cracking open all my defenses. My wolf preens inside me, begging for more than his gaze on me.

His broad shoulders rise and fall in a long sigh. "I was a fool to break our bond. I knew the pack couldn't forgive you, and it's my job to protect them. I have to lead, but that doesn't mean I don't want you, too."

His head cocks to the side as he says this, as if measuring my response. The vulnerability he's sharing with me must come hard. Alphas, I've learned, aren't keen on letting people see them as less than anything other than the strongest, most dominant leaders. The fact that he's opening up to me means a lot. But it doesn't undo what he did.

"It was a pretty stupid move," I concede. "You could have told me about the vampires before I left here."

"You didn't give me that option," he says, sounding frustrated. "You ran out of here. I tried to find you, but your scent trail just... ended."

"That must be when Evan carried me," I ponder aloud.

Axel nods, looking miserable. "I should have heard you out."

"Yeah," I say. "You should have. You did everything so fast. You brought me here, and threw me in with the pack at that horrible dinner, and then the mating part—well, that part I liked, but then it... Scared me. I didn't even know you, and I felt more bound to you than to my own mama."

"I know," he says, lifting his hands in the air. "I acted rashly, which is exactly why I need a submissive around to help calm me and slow me down. I'm too alpha for my own good. But I can admit I made a huge-ass mistake. I still feel the bond, though, Luna. It might have been dissolved, but it's still here. Isn't it?"

He studies me, his eyes filled with pleading and hope that makes my resolve soften.

I cross my arms over my chest and look past him so I won't give in, even though he's not using even a trace of his dominant wolf energy on me.

"Look, Luna, I get it," he says, reaching over and gently laying his hand over mine. "We can never be True Mates again, and that's something I have to live with, because it's the biggest mistake of my life and it always will be. But maybe, if you'd give me another chance, I could make it up to you. I could still be your mate."

I eye him warily. "How?"

"By being your mate," he says. "We can rule the pack together, side by side, how it always should have been. We can get married and have pups. I'll protect you with my life, Luna. I'll never let anything hurt you again. And we'll be bonded, not just the pack bond, but a special mate bond. We'll be able to hear each other's thoughts. I can always see if you're in danger."

If I'd never met the triplets, the idea might appeal to me. But now thoughts of them flow through my body like blood.

"What about Ama?" I ask.

"Ama's too dominant to be a match for me," he says without hesitation. "We bring out the worst in each other, not the best. You, though… You bring out the best."

"So after everything, you still want me," I marvel. "You want me to stay and be your mate, ruling the pack side by side."

His Adam's apple bobs up and down as he stares at my lips with a yearning expression. "More than anything."

I stare at his lips as he leans forward, so close I feel his warm breath on my lips. My heart flutters in my chest, and something hot flutters between my thighs, and my wolf whines with longing. When his lips connect with mine, more confusion swamps my brain. He doesn't taste or feel anything like the other two men I've kissed. His chin is smooth instead of scratchy with a beard, but his lips are warm and tender as they connect with mine. He scoots in, moving his head in a slow, sensuous circle, his hand cradling my head. My body floods with heat and desire.

Cars roll by on the street outside the window, making the wet thwack, thwack, thwack noise that all cars make around here. A motorcycle roars past, and I'm suddenly filled with longing for the triplets and their motorcycles. A tear escapes from my eye as I think of Callan, Warrick, and Ethan. I pull away from Axel and regard his hooded gaze.

His lips are shiny, his breath coming as quick as mine.

"Was that a yes?" he asks, hope shining in his eyes.

My wolf urges me to say yes, but my human isn't on board. No matter how good he makes my body feel, my heart belongs to three others. I swallow and shake my head. "No, Axel. I'm not your mate anymore, and I never will be."

# **Chapter Four**

*Axel*

Luna's denial crushes my lungs so hard I can't take a breath. After she answers, she scurries away from the table and races upstairs, as if she can't bear to see my face. I pace the floor, prowling through the house that should be ours to fill with children and nice things, but instead is a lonely, dusty bachelor pad without Luna.

At last, I climb the stairs to the second floor and knock on the door of the room I prepared for her. I'm met with stony silence. At least I know she's still in there because even a wolf can't jump from the second-floor window without being injured in the fall. I can hear her on the other side of the door, anyway, can smell her and sense her presence just out of reach. Her wolf calls to mine, and my wolf roars for me to tear down the door and go to her, claim her fully this time. I fucked her during our mate bonding, but I never came, and my wolf is tormented with the memory that our claiming was never completed. He wants Luna, wants to claim every part of her to the depths of our wolf spirits.

Today, it took every ounce of willpower I possess to let her come on my cock without fucking her into the ground the way I wanted. But I had to gain her compliance, and pleasure is the only offer she's responded to so far. I had to show her that I can control her pleasure without forcing her submission. I want it given willingly.

Fuck, what I wouldn't give to ravish her sweet little body, though, now so much more womanly and appealing than when we found her in the swamp, half-starved and on her own.

When she refuses to open the door, I plod back downstairs. I've got to do something to get out of my head and end the torment she's filled me with. I grab my phone and tap in Ama's number.

"Yes, boss?" she says on the third ring.

"I need you to watch my house and keep an eye on Luna," I say. The pack is about to rebel over my reckless decision to get her back, and I'm not about to lose her already. I have to convince her that this is where she belongs and convince them that she's worth what I gave up.

"Do I have permission to kill her if needed?" Ama asks with a sassy tone to her voice.

"No, you don't have permission to fucking kill her. You're not to harm a hair on her head."

"You're the boss," she says, then hangs up.

A few minutes later, Ama strolls in, not bothering to knock. She flashes me a simpering gaze, then sidles up next to me. "What's wrong, Alpha? Trouble in paradise?"

"Nothing I can't handle," I snap, not wanting to involve her in my personal life. She's already wormed her way into it more than I like. Appeasing my Second helps keep her happy, which helps keep the pack running smoothly, but Ama pushes my boundaries every chance she gets.

"You shouldn't have brought her back," she says. "But you know that, don't you?"

"It's already been done."

"Let me stand by your side," she says. "If you gave it a shot, you'd see how good we can be together. How well we can rule. Luna's nothing but a whelp. She'll never understand pack politics." Her palm lands on my bicep, and she scratches her nails gently against my skin, giving me an inviting look. I know she's down to fuck, that she's hoping I'll give in when I get too frustrated, the way I have before. She doesn't seem to understand that's all it will ever be.

"You're not to talk about my mate disparagingly," I say, brushing her hand from my arm. I slide past her and grab my keys from the hook next to the door. "Stay here until I get back. Do not leave under any circumstances. If Luna needs something, get it for her. She's allowed anything she wants, but don't let her leave. If she tries, contact me through our pack bond. I'll be back soon."

Ama glowers at me, but I don't care. She, Luna, and everyone I know will be better off if I run this out of my system.

I drive like the Devil's on my tail, heading to Creebay Preserve. Once there, I park, shift into my wolfskin, and head into the swamp. Anything but centered, I only chase instead of catching this evening. I already ate, so I don't need to catch anything. I just need to hunt, to run and feel the wind in my fur, my powerful body racing through the preserve. When I'm utterly and thoroughly exhausted, I head back to the truck, shift to my human form, and drive back home.

On the drive back, I can't stop thinking of Luna. She's taken up space in every cell in my body. I can still taste the sweet nectar of her cum when I knelt over her today, and she lay there unashamed, with her legs spread while I took in the sight of her glorious, well-pleased body lying limp before me. With every breath I inhale, I breathe her into me. Every exhale, I try to let her go. The constant, maddening push and pull is driving me mad.

I'm furious I gave away so much land to get her back, and now it's all for nothing. Her rejection lances my heart like a blunt arrow-tip, shredding my muscles and organs as it burrows its way through my chest. What do I have left? We have only a bit more than half the land we had yesterday, and I have nothing to show for it. I gave away pack territory without consulting the pack, and I got nothing in return for the sacrifice. This impulsive, selfish decision will carry severe consequences.

When I arrive back at the house, I'm almost as twisted up again as I was when I left.

Ama is sprawled across my sofa, staring at the television with a bored expression on her face. "Hey, Axel," she says, picking up the remote and shutting the TV off.

"Any sign of Luna?" I say, hanging my keys on the hook.

"I heard the toilet flush about an hour ago, and then she must have gone to bed, because I haven't heard a peep out of her since." She swings her legs from the coffee table and rises to her feet. "Am I dismissed now?"

"Yes. Thank you for caring for Luna."

"I don't give a fuck about her," she says, fishing her keys from the pocket of her shorts. "I only did it for you."

"Thanks again," I say.

"Anything for you," Ama coos, stepping in to wrap her arms around me. I start to detach myself, but I've been such as asshole since I lost Luna that I should probably start making amends. So, I submit to her embrace—until she starts grinding her body against mine like she's trying to see if she can get me hard.

I untangle myself from her and step back, putting a healthy amount of distance between us.

"I'm with Luna," I remind her.

With a huff, she whirls around and storms out.

I don't have time for her ridiculous infatuation, so I lock the door and head upstairs to shower. I'm in the middle of rinsing off when the lights blink out. From the darkness outside the small window, I know it's another blackout, something that happens on the regular in these parts. Probably another powerline swallowed into a sinkhole.

With a sigh, I finish rinsing off in the dark and climb out of the shower. We'll be left to wait in the dark until the city decides to restore the grid. I towel off and then remember what Ama said—that she hadn't heard a noise from Luna in hours.

My chest does a funny little squeeze, and I almost lose my breath at the thought that maybe she tried to escape out the window after all. Tucking my towel around my hips, I sneak down the hall and press my ear to her door. When they say "lovesick," they've got it right, because this is an illness I can't seem to shake.

I can't hear anything but deep breathing, so she must be asleep. But I have to know for sure, have to see with my own eyes that she's here, in our home. Slowly, I turn the door handle to her room. It doesn't make a sound as it unlatches. I open the door and wait for a shoe to be thrown at me or maybe one of the kitchen knives. When she doesn't hurl anything my way, I step into the bedroom I set up just for her, knowing she'd want her own space.

"Luna," I whisper in the darkness, turning over the beautiful word in my mouth, my fingers curling against the urge to touch her soft skin, to make sure she's real.

I've seen she's here, and I know I should leave, but I can't seem to go. I have to be near her.

She doesn't move, just lies there with the sheet over her rising and falling with each breath. I step closer, standing over her and watching her breathe. Her plump lips are parted, her lashes curling against her cheek, a picture of sweet innocence. I pull the sheet up, covering her shoulder. She sighs and gives a sexy little moan, rolling onto her back. The sheet slides from her body, leaving her gloriously naked, the outlines of her curves visible in the faint moonlight streaming in the window.

I swallow hard, trying not to gape at her body, at the way her legs are slightly spread, her shaved pussy bare and scented like the sweetest nectar. My mouth waters, and my cock throbs. I made her come twice today, but I want to taste her now, to lick her until I've had my fill of her and she's come on my face. I remember how much she liked that the first time we were together.

She was thinner then, with more hair. Why the fuck is her pussy shaved now? Is she fucking the filthy outlaws she's been living with? That has to be it. How else would she even know to do that? I've heard the rumors in town, how they fight the men at the rough bars on that side of town and fuck their way through all the women they can get their dicks in. Rage pulses in my temples. They have no right to touch the likes of my sweet Luna.

Before I can think about it, I step forward and lower myself between her open legs. I just want to see her better. As softly as I can, I press my palms to the tops of her inner thighs and spread her open. My cock throbs, and my wolf growls for more. I can smell her sweet cunt, how wet it smells, like it flows with the nectar of the gods. Closing my eyes, I lean down and take a long, deep breath, inhaling her fragrance that makes my wolf go mad inside me. He still thinks she's our True Mate.

I wrestle for control as he roars to get free, to have at her. Leaning down, I promise him just a taste. I let the very tip of my tongue touch her. The taste of her invades me, takes me over. Unable to stop myself, I sweep my tongue along her inner folds and circle her clit. Excitement flares in my belly and cock like I'm on a good hunt, but the reward is a thousand times better than the first bite of fresh blood.

I let my tongue linger at her clit, pressing lightly until I feel it throb in response. She lets out a moan and murmurs sleepily. She's mine, and when she's not fighting it tooth and claw, she wants me to claim her. My wolf feels hers calling to him, to us, wanting us as much as we want her.

She shifts her hips, angling her pelvis toward my mouth. That's all the invitation I need. I slide my tongue as deep as it will go inside her. She moans, and I feast on her sweet pussy, licking her with more insistence, sucking and thrusting my tongue into her snug little hole.

She grips the sheets suddenly, jerking beneath my mouth. "What are you doing?" she hisses.

"I'm making you feel good," I say, my voice a moan of torment. "Don't you like it?"

A beat of silence meets my ears, and I hesitate before continuing.

"Yes," she finally whispers, her head falling back on the pillow.

It's the best word I've heard all day—hell, it's the best word I've heard since she ran from my house the first time. I dive back in, determined to give her pleasure until she can't bear it. I thrust my tongue deep inside her, fucking her tight cunt until she moans and buries her hand in my hair, pulling me in and opening her legs wide to let me go deeper. I want to slam my cock into her, fuck her until she screams for more. But this isn't about me.

When her slick coats my tongue and she comes, I can hardly contain myself. She cries out in wordless pleasure, bucking under me. At last, she sinks back to the bed. But I'm just getting started.

I begin again, drawing back and moving to her clit, swirling my tongue around it to build her back up as she pants and whimpers, helpless against the pleasure I can give. I suck and nibble her lovely pearl while sliding a finger into her juicy entrance. After a minute, she starts to buck against me, and I add another finger, feeling the snug but delicious stretch of her cunt. I work a third one in, and she gasps and cries out, her hips writhing as I ease the third finger deeper, until it's gripped with the others inside her hot, slick entrance.

The sight makes me lightheaded, and I let my other hand roam her body, caressing her silky skin, fondling her breasts, then pinching her nipple between my thumb and finger. She lets out a mewling cry, and I begin to thrust my fingers deep inside her dripping pussy as hard as I can. Then I lean down, licking her slippery clit before latching on and suckling at it. She shrieks as she comes hard, thrashing under me like a wild animal as her walls clench around my fingers and her clit throbs against my tongue over and over.

She falls back with a long moan afterwards. Her body shudders, and her grip on my fingers loosens. I slide my hand from between her legs and lick her cum from my fingers like I did before, licking my lips and savoring the taste and smell of her on my face. The connection of our wolves thrums between us, as if they were never separated, as if they can't be. I crawl up the bed and lay beside her, wrapping my arms around her. She's still breathing hard, and her skin is misted with a sheen of sweat.

"You liked that, didn't you?" I ask, knowing full well that she did. But I want her to admit it aloud, so she has to hear it for herself.

"Yes," she breathes.

I stroke her silken breasts, fingering her nipples into tight buds and relishing the way she sucks in a breath.

"I'll make you feel this good every day," I promise. "I'll do anything for you, Luna, without asking for anything in return. I just want you to be mine, to give you all the pleasure you deserve. It won't even be a sacrifice to forgo my own orgasm. Pleasuring you is all I need. Having you here is all I need."

I wait for her to answer, to say anything, hating that I need her to agree so fucking badly. But I don't push. As I remain by her side, waiting for her to answer, I continue to massage and caress her breasts, belly, waist, and hips. My cock is so hard I could explode, but I won't ask for anything from her. I will only give until she wants to give back.

Finally, she rolls to her side and faces me. "You've said that a couple of times—that you'll do anything for me."

Soft light glimmers in her eyes as she regards me.

"I did. And I meant every word. What do you want, my love?" I reach for her hand and press her knuckles against my lips.

"Anything at all?" she says.

"Anything."

"What if you don't like it?"

"I don't have to like it. I only care that you're happy and at my side."

"If you want me to be happy…"

"I do," I say firmly. "What do you need, Luna love?" I scoot closer and kiss her neck, her collarbone, and the top of her breasts.

"I want to go home," she says. "Back to the triplets."

# Chapter Five

*Luna*

"No," Axel says flatly, rolling away from me, onto his back. I can feel his wolf raging inside him, though, and mine cowers. Somehow, by some wolf bond, she can feel how irate he is at my request. Axel the man may be keeping himself under control, but his wolf is wild with fury, and I can only imagine how hard it must be for him to control it right now. He's so strong, stronger than anyone I've ever met, to contain that level of wolf fury. The mattress vibrates from the energy pouring out of him, but he doesn't move a muscle to tear me apart like his wolf wants to.

Still, I feel like I'm going to be shoved through the wall from the force of his wolf's anger.

I shrink away from him, covering my face with my hands. "Okay," I say meekly, pulling my knees up to my chest to protect myself from his wolf's outrage, in case it gets loose.

"Shit," he groans. "You can feel that, can't you? My wolf?" He turns to me, and I can feel him watching in the near darkness, though my hands are still over my face. "I can feel yours. That I've scared you."

I nod mutely.

"Fuck," he mutters. "Luna, I'd never hurt you. Neither would my wolf. I promise."

He strokes my hair with his palm before trying to pry my hands from my face.

"Luna," he says, his voice coaxing me to come out. "I was surprised at your request, that's all. After today... I thought you'd reconsider. You asked to mate. That means something."

"It does?" I ask from the shield of my hands.

He lets out a breath of laughter. "Yes, Luna. It does. To me, at least, it does."

"What does it mean?" I ask into my palms."

"It means… I want to be your mate. That I thought you wanted to be mine again when you said you'd let me fuck you."

"Oh," I whisper, remembering what the triplets said about choosing and jealousy. I didn't choose Axel. I just like the way he makes me feel so good I think I'll die, and the way my wolf feels cozy and warm when he's near.

"Please take your hands away from your face," he says gently. "I'm sorry I scared you. And I'm sorry I can't give you what you want. Anything else in the world, yes. But not that."

I shake my head. "That's all I want."

Axel sighs and rolls onto his back next to me. "I'm sorry."

I peek through my fingers at his expression. Even though it's nightfall, the moon outside the house lends enough light to witness his misery.

A chasm of silence swallows the two of us in its embrace.

"Let's go hunting," he says at last.

"Maybe," I say through my fingers, my heart speeding with excitement at the thought. The triplets told me not to leave the area around their house when they weren't home, and aside from checking Callan's traps a few times before that, I haven't been out and let my wolf really run since before leaving the swamps. The thought of a hunt has my wolf yipping for joy inside me.

"Not the whole pack," Axel says, sounding more excited, too. "Just the two of us."

"Really?" I ask, cautiously lowering my hands.

"We usually hunt as a pack, since it's a bonding experience that unifies us. But it'll be good for us, and I need to work off some of this frustration."

"Frustration that I want to leave?" I ask.

"Sure," he says with a little smirk.

I feel like I'm missing something, but I don't know what else he could be frustrated about.

I let my legs unfold from my torso. "Okay. I'd like that."

"That's my girl," he says, clearly pleased. "We'll go at dawn. That's the best time."

My wolf preens at his praise, even when I try to quell her excitement. I allow her the comfort of his arms, though, and let him pull me in and hold me while we fall asleep. I dream of Callan, Warrick, and Ethan. In my dream, I'm wading through water to get to them but as soon as I get close, a storm pushes them away.

When I wake, Axel is gone, and I'm groggy despite sleeping all day yesterday. A hunt will do me some good. I pad downstairs, excited by the prospect.

After coffee, toast, and eggs prepared by Axel, we drive off to the preserve. The skies are dark, and the clouds hang bloated with their liquid offspring. It reminds me of my dream last night, and I wonder how the triplets are preparing for the storm.

As the truck speeds out of the neighborhood, I turn to Axel. "Can I ask you a question?"

He glances at me, then nods and returns his gaze to the road.

"Why isn't Ama your mate? Ethan told me more about True Mates, so I know you can't choose that. But since we're no longer True Mates without the bond, you can choose anyone as a regular mate. Why choose me, after you went to all that trouble and pain to get rid of me? Ama is here already, she knows the pack, and she wants to be your mate something fierce."

"I told you. Ama's too dominant to be my mate," Axel says. "She doesn't temper my impulsiveness. We work well together, but we're not suitable mates."

I think of them leading together, the way he said he and I would if I was his mate, and my chest gets all tight and funny. I wish I could go back to my men, where I didn't have to think about anything else and didn't have to know about leading a pack.

Thinking about them makes the ache in my chest even deeper. Not wanting to bring brooding energy to the hunt today, I try to shake these thoughts out of my system. Hunting is fun and exciting, a way to catch food, and a way to let our wolves take charge for a while. It's rejuvenating and as essential as being in our human form sometimes.

"Let's hunt Key deer," Axel says, seeming to sense my mood. "You ever caught one of those?"

"I don't know," I admit. "I got a few deer before, but I don't know the names of them."

"They're smaller than a regular deer," Axel says. "They used to only live in the Keys, but the hurricanes and storms flooded the islands, and they swam north to the mainland. The ones that survived and made it to land spread out and migrated throughout the southeast. We'll have to coordinate our hunting efforts because they're smart."

"Good thing we're smart, too," I say, offering him a little smile.

"They aren't usually taken down without a good chase, but that's exactly what we want—a good chase, right?" Axel grins, and my wolf does that swelling-up thing in my chest, like it would when I did something that made Mama real proud of me.

"Yeah," I say, turning to the window to hide my giddiness. "I haven't hunted for weeks."

The truck bumps and jostles over a section of road marred by potholes. I stare out the window at all the dilapidated buildings sinking into oneness with the earth.

Living with Mama in Bogbeast Waters, I never encountered city buildings. I only first saw one when Ama dragged me to Jacksonville to mate with Axel. Sure, sometimes we'd find the remnants of a house, but more often than not, we just found stuff washed up in the bog. When we ventured far enough to happen on an old homestead, Mama would say it was time to turn around and head home. She said old houses have bad juju. But I'd go back on my own sometimes and get things we could use. They never brought any kind of juju.

"Weeks, huh?" Axel says, reaching for my hand and squeezing it. "That's too long for a wolf."

I let my hand go limp as a dead swamp rat in his, and Axel sighs and pulls back.

"Tell me how you'd hunt with your mama," Axel says.

That brightens me up, and I sit up straight in my seat. "The deer we hunted traveled in small herds. They'd try to outrun us, but that was when we'd keep 'em running, so we could find out who's the weakest or the oldest. That's the one we'd separate from the others. If it happened to be a male, then watch out, Mama! Their antlers could gore us real bad or gut us on the spot."

I bounce in the seat, starting to get caught up in the thrill of the hunt.

"That's right," Axel says, with a broad grin. "That's exactly what we'll do today. Once we've found our mark, we have to flank the deer on either side. If we both stay on the same side, it'll get away from us. We'll surround it and keep pace. When it starts to wear itself out, you go for a hind leg. When the deer stumbles, I'll go for the throat. That's my role on the hunt."

Axel pulls off on some gravel on the side of the road, and we toss our clothes into the truck and shift into our wolfskins. I'm practically dancing with excitement. Axel jumps on me, startling me, and we roll over and over in the grass together. I finally break free and skip away, shaking off to get the dirt and grass out of my fur. Axel's tongue lolls out happily, and he pounces at me again.

This time, I hop out of the way, then grab him with my front legs. We tip over, rolling in the grass and playing for a few more minutes, nipping and yipping and pouncing on each other. Even though he's twice my size and he's the Alpha, Axel even lets me pin him on the ground a couple times. When I was a pup, Mama used to play wolf games with me, but as I grew older, she got more and more into her own mind and snapped at me if I tried to engage her in play, so I stopped trying.

I forgot how much I liked it—needed it. It feels like I've been starving for years and finally fed my wolf soul. By the time Axel gets up and lopes into the woods, my wolf is so happy I think she'll turn into pure sunlight.

Axel's nose keeps skimming the earth as we trot through the woods. I don't know what he's sniffing for, but I sniff, too. I take in all the scents of those who have traversed this land—rabbits and rats, snakes and lizards, even a big old gator. I come across a wolf scent, and my heart soars. I linger at the spot, trying to figure out who it belongs to. Is it one of the triplets, or do all wolves share this smell?

Axel doubles around and checks out what I'm doing. He politely sniffs, too, then turns away and bumps me with his shoulder, indicating I should follow. Some faint stirring tickles my brain as if he's trying to communicate with me, wolf to wolf, but I can't hear more than his emotions, since I'm not bonded into the pack to hear his thoughts. Maybe he's saying, "This is wolf territory—get used to it."

Since I can't really pick up his communication, I leave my investigation and trot behind him. Deeper in the marsh, Axel pauses, lifts his head, and scents something. I follow his lead and catch a familiar animal smell—the deer. My adrenaline kicks in, and I fight the urge to lift my muzzle and howl. It's just us, so there's no use in calling, though, just like when it was me and Mama.

Axel trots ahead and pauses, looking back over his shoulder at me and then ahead through some shrubbery at a clearing. I spot a herd of little deer, and a wave of excitement ripples through me. I know Axel feels it, too. He gets low in a semi-crouch, then bursts into the clearing.

The deer scatter, and the chase is on!

I keep an eye on Axel's movements, but my wolf instinct tells me all I need to know. We run beside and behind the frightened deer as they seek safety in the forest. A couple of deer stumble and fall back, but then they catch up with the others.

Axel cuts one of the stumblers away from the herd. It starts to panic and bleat, making wild, panicked sounds of alarm.

A buck doubles back and sets to attack Axel, antlers down. It makes a couple of quick snorts, followed by a hoof stomp. Axel charges and retreats, charges and retreats, careful to duck out of the way of the buck's sharp, spearing antlers.

I try to corral the young deer Axel set as our target by lunging back and forth, my exhilaration building. But the deer makes a bolt for it and scrambles away to join the safety of the herd.

Disappointed in myself, I head towards Axel.

He's still warring with the buck.

I guess we're going to feast on a male deer. I creep up behind the buck, who still has its eye on Axel.

The buck whirls on me at the last second, but I jet out of the way.

Axel nips at its hind leg, and it pivots to attack him instead.

I leap for its haunches, my teeth connecting, only to be nailed in the neck by its other rear leg. I yelp and scramble out of the way. Blood streams from the deer's hindquarters as it spins to charge me. The smell is intoxicating and sends me even higher into attack mode.

Axel darts in to take another chunk from the deer's rear. He's quicker than I am when the buck strikes out, narrowly missing his head. But now the buck has two injuries, and it's limping, clearly in pain. It circles around to Axel, and I charge toward it and seize the back thigh. The buck falters, and its rear legs give way.

Axel goes for the kill, tearing into the neck of our prey as it huffs its last breath. His teeth land solid, and he shakes and rips the deer's throat out. Then he tears apart its belly with his powerful jaws. I crawl toward the fallen deer, but some instinct tells me to wait for my Alpha to feast before I begin. I sit on my haunches, my tongue lolling out as I pant with eagerness, a high whine escaping unbidden. It smells so good I'm drooling.

Axel rips out the liver and chomps it down. Then, he rips and tears at the diaphragm, making room for his muzzle. Once he has access to the chest cavity, he shoves his nose inside and goes for the heart. He pulls it free of the chest and steps over, gently setting it on the ground at my feet. I know it's the best part, a precious prize that he's honoring me with. I feel like the highest of all beings as I lean in and rub my face along Axel's crimson one, licking the blood from his fur. It's salty and delicious on my tongue, and I clean him for another minute before stepping back to consume the prize he's given me.

I can feel the pride rolling off Axel, that he thinks we did good, that we make a good hunting team. I can't deny it, and I feel myself preening under his attention. I know the gift of the heart is more than a reward for being a good hunter, though. It's a precious sacrifice he's making, showing me that I deserve the best, even better than what he had. That he'll put me first.

When I'm done, Axel nudges me, and together we turn back to the small animal. I tear the fur away from the hind leg's muscles and eat the delicious meat. It's a lesser prize than the liver or heart, but I'm in feast mode, and my wolf is the happiest she's been in a long, long time.

We feast as other carnivores—crows, a small fox, a buzzard or two—circle around, waiting for the leftovers. A couple of times, Axel has to chase away the bold ones who try to pick at the meat before we're finished. I stand over the kill, admiring his power and finesse, my wolf swelling with pride and adoration as he skillfully defends what is ours.

When we're both glutted and happy, Axel trots away, looks over his shoulder at me, and gestures for me to follow him. We head through the woods for a few minutes before emerging at a spring, steam rising from the warm water. We both leap into the pool, splash about and lap the warm, mineral-infused water.

Axel approaches me and begins to lick my neck—the place where the buck kicked me. It feels so soothing to be nurtured by someone. I've been the caregiver to Mama since I came of age six years ago, and being cared for is like a sweet memory of childhood. I fall into a lull, eyes half-closed, as Axel licks and cleans my wounds.

Something makes my fur stand on end, though, and I turn and sniff the air, scanning the trees at the same time. I can smell another wolf. Someone is watching us, I just know it. A flicker of movement catches my attention in the trees, and I whip my head back around, my ears pricked. Suddenly, Mama's words come back to me.

*Wolves are the enemy. They'll betray you. Never trust a wolf.*

Is someone watching us? And who? Did Axel ask Ama to come along in case I attacked him and tried to escape, like he did last night when he left? And if it's not her, then who is it? Could it be Mama's ghost keeping an eye on me, watching over me, reminding me not to give in no matter how good it feels to have Axel's tongue cleaning my wound?

The thought of Mama coming back to warn me sends shivers through my soul. Add the fear of being watched to the mantra she instilled in me—never trust the wolves—and I know I need to get away. I scramble from the hot spring and bolt into the woods in a panic, trying to shake off the spell of contentment of being with Axel, so I can remember that he's not safe. He hurt me

and my wolf, no matter how good he makes us feel now.
I need to get away before I forget that he's the enemy.

# **Chapter Six**

*Luna*

I know better than to think I can escape a more muscular, older wolf, but I still run. I'm acting on wolf instinct, not human logic. I dodge shrubs, leap over stones, splash through a marshy area. I can feel eyes on me, can smell a wolf, but when I look over my shoulder, I see nothing but the shadowy forest. Did Axel let me go, or did I somehow manage to escape?

A sense of giddiness crashes against the fear rippling through my body at the thought of him chasing me again, like he did outside the vampire's lair.

Then guilt tugs at my heart, because as much as my body and my wolf adore Axel, my heart still belongs to the three men who saved me when Axel didn't—who saved me from what he did to me.

*I'll find my way back. I can do it.*

I glance over my shoulder again, and finding no one in pursuit, I slow my frenetic pace. But when my head swings forward again, my heart leaps into my throat. Axel bears down on me, his teeth pulled back in a snarl.

The bastard got ahead of me!

Before I can even swerve out of the way, he tackles me. We tumble over and over until coming to a stop in a patch of pine needles. I'm soaked from the spring, breathing hard and turned around from rolling head over tail so many times, but have enough wits about me to feel Axel's jaw clamped around my neck.

I close my eyes, waiting for him to rip my throat out or use his Alpha dominance to make me behave, the way Warrick would. Instead, I feel his body shift on mine, and his human hand begins to stroke my neck and head, rubbing around my ears, soothing me. "Luna love," he croons. "You've got to learn to trust me. I won't hurt you, but I'm not letting you get away again. You are mine, Luna. You can run to the ends of the earth, and I'll find you and claim you as many times as you need me to until you understand that."

His words make my wolf side thrill with joy, but they settle uneasily in my belly, where my human side balks in protest. I snap at his hand.

He yanks it away and leaps to his feet. "Go on then." He points toward the trees. "Run, my little mate. I'm happy to chase you a thousand times because I know I'll catch you and carry you home to warm my bed at the end of the day."

I lie there panting, considering my options. I will never outrun the Alpha who is so insistent on claiming me and making up for rejecting me to begin with. But if he's enlisted the help of his Second to watch us, that means he thinks I'm a threat. That I could hurt him enough to escape, if not kill him. I don't hate him the way I did at first, not enough to want him dead, but I do want the freedom to make my own choices. And if that means fighting my way out, I'm not afraid of getting my paws dirty.

I scramble to my feet and lunge for Axel, teeth bared, but he's too quick for me. He darts aside, and in the few seconds it takes for me to turn around and leap back to where he is, he's shifted back into his fur.

He goes for my throat again. When I'm pinned once more, he holds my throat in his powerful jaws, his fangs squeezing but not breaking the skin. A low growl rumbles in his throat.

We remain like this for several long minutes until I shift back to human. He shifts, too, and suddenly we're both naked against one another, glaring at each other like we could bite the other's head off like a catfish headed for the supper table.

"Get off me," I snarl, pushing against his rigid body.

"Are you going to run again?"

"Maybe," I say, refusing to look away.

He positions his forearm against my collarbones. "Then I'm not going anywhere."

"Get off. You're too heavy." I curl my fingers around the muscles of his arm, and he eases up, but he doesn't release me.

"Want to play chase again?" he asks, a smile curling his lips that makes me want to rip his face off.

"This isn't funny," I snap, seething with fury. "You had your chance to claim me, Axel. I could have been yours. But now I'm not, and that was your choice, not mine."

"How many times are you going to remind me?" he says, sorrow washing over his face.

"As many as it takes." I jerk my head up and bite his shoulder.

His jaw clenches, but he says nothing. "Admit it. We were having fun before you got spooked. What happened?"

I shake my head, unwilling to share.

He huffs out a sigh. "Have it your way. I'll wear you down until you trust me one of these days."

"You threw me away," I snarl.

"We've already established that. And now I'm trying to correct my mistake," Axel says, nuzzling my cheek with his nose.

"It's too late," I snap. "I found other men who wanted me, even when I didn't know how to use a fork. And I want them. Let me go home."

He stills, and his eyes narrow. "That's not your home."

"You can't keep me away from them," I say, pushing against his solid muscles.

"Want to bet?" he growls.

I spit in his face, struggling under him, but he doesn't budge, and the more I struggle, the more I can feel his cock hardening against my thigh.

"Let me go," I cry.

"Did you let them fuck you?" His voice is low and sharp, like a ragged blade.

"What if I did?" I writhe beneath him, and the sand and pine needles scrape against my backside.

"That's not an answer. It's a question. Did you let those bastards fuck you?" His face has transformed into steel and edges.

I reach up with both hands and shove against him. "Why do you care?"

"I care," he growls.

I stare up through the leaves overhead at the gray sky. It still looks like it's going to storm, but maybe it's biding its time just like I am, plotting my escape to find my lovers. What is the right way to get back to them? How can I get Axel to give me up? If I say yes, maybe he will think I don't belong to him anymore.

I stare into his eyes, the color of agates. He seems to carry the weight of the ages in his gaze. My wolf shimmers inside me the way she does when her fur wants to rise at the lonesome howls we used to hear from the pack when we lived in Bogbeast Waters. Mama would always hurry us inside when they were hunting.

Axel's body feels like a thousand tons, his cock like a steel rod against me, though he doesn't seem to notice. The sensation of it makes heat and wetness build between my legs.

Axel puts pressure on my chest and repeats, "Did. You. Fuck. Them?"

"One of them," I say, lifting my chin and glaring at him.

Axel reaches down with his free hand and strokes my mound. "Is that why you shaved your pussy?"

A smile lights my face at the memory of Ethan climbing in the tub with me. "No," I say. "I didn't shave it."

Axel's eyes flash, and I can feel his wolf's fury inside him even if his human tries to hide it. "Who shaved you?" he growls, pushing a finger inside my slick entrance.

"One of the others," I say, my breath coming quicker. I watch the way he flinches, and some mean little part of me is happy about that. I know that dissolving our bond hurt him as much as it hurt me, but the difference is, he chose it anyway. I would never have chosen to hurt him that way.

"One of them fucked you, one of them shaved you... What did the third one do?" His breath lands hot on my face and neck, and his cock pulses against my thigh as he thrusts his finger into me more roughly.

I gasp and open my thighs, pushing my pussy into his hand.

"Answer me, Luna," he growls in that same sharp-edged voice. He drives a second finger into me. "What did you let the last one do? Did you let him lick this sweet cunt like I did last night? Or are they too proud to eat pussy?"

"Nothing," I whisper, thinking of how Callan dyed my hair and pushed his cock up against me until we both nearly exploded.

"It doesn't look like nothing," Axel says. "It doesn't feel like nothing. Your cunt's dripping for them."

"He didn't do anything." My gaze whips toward Axel, and anger replaces memory of Callan. "What's it to you? They saved me after you—"

"Believe me, I know what I did," Axel growls, grinding his cock into my thigh while his fingers pump relentlessly into my slick tightness. "I get to be tortured by you every fucking day. How could I forget?"

"Tortured? How am I torturing you?" I buck my hips, panting for more. He's torturing me by not letting me find my satisfaction.

He groans and buries his fingers deep inside me. "You're hot one minute, icy-cold the next. I'm going out of my mind, Luna. I want to fuck you so hard you forget they ever existed."

His eyes are wild, his fingers stroking the spot inside me that makes me nearly lose my mind. Just when I think I'll burst, he withdraws his fingers.

I fight back a cry of protest.

"Did you like fucking them?" he asks.

My eyes fly wide. "What?"

"Did you like it when those assholes fucked you?" Making tiny thrusts with his hips, he's breathing through his mouth now, shallow and fast like me as his shaft slides against my slick folds.

"Maybe I did," I say.

A twig cracks in the woods, and I listen hard. Axel doesn't seem to notice—he's too distracted with grinding against my wet pussy.

"Stop fucking around and answer the question," he snaps.

"Fine," I say. "Yes, I loved being fucked by him. Is that what you wanted to hear? Now, would you please get off me? I've got sticks and leaves poking against me, sand grinding against my skin, and you're heavy."

"Are you going to run? Because I will catch you, little mouse. And you might not like what happens then."

"Why not?"

"Because I'll reclaim you, and you won't belong to that mutt any longer."

He pushes up off me, standing to hold out his hand to me. I take it, stand, and start to knee him between the legs, but he's too quick for me, as if he expected no less. He grabs my arm and whips me around, so my back is facing him and my arm is bent behind my back.

"Let me go!" I howl.

"Never," he hisses in my ear.

I stomp on his foot.

"You wanna play this way, huh? You like it rough, is that it? Have I been too nice to you?" He marches me forward, his cock jabbing into my back with each step.

Another twig snaps in the woods, and I know someone's watching us, though I don't know who. A little thrill races through me, and it's not fear. I hope it's Ama, that she can see how much Axel wants me. I arch my back, pushing my backside against him. Axel pushes me away from him, and I start to run. I don't get three steps before he grabs me from behind, pushing me up against a tree instead of taking me to the ground.

"I hate you," I snarl, shoving my hips against his, aching for him to quench the fire blazing inside me. He got me going and then left me undone.

He crouches slightly and then slams upwards, ramming his cock inside me with one brutal thrust. I cry out in shock and pleasure and pain, and he thrusts into me again.

"If you hate me, then why are you so fucking wet every time I touch you?" he growls, pumping his thick cock into me so hard I can barely breathe through the pleasure crashing over me.

I can't even begin to form words to answer him. My breasts and face will be scraped to shit by the bark, but I don't care. I want him inside of me, need him to feed my wolf this ecstasy that he gives me every time. He grabs my hair and twists my head to the side, pushing my cheek into the rough tree bark. Then, he bites my neck. I can smell the blood, and it makes me writhe and buck with madness, but he only slams harder and harder into me. I feel a burning stretch near my entrance, but I don't know what's happening, why it feels like he's getting bigger inside me. I just know I have to keep going.

"Fuck," he says, suddenly, pulling out.

"What?" I ask, stumbling away from the tree in a daze.

"I'm knotting," he says. "It only happens with a True Mate."

I look down at the swelling that bulges at the base of his cock, the one I started to feel right before he stopped. "What does that mean?" I ask.

"You'll see," he says, pulling me back to him, a determined look in his eye. He seizes the back of my thighs, lifts me up, and impales me with his erection. I can feel a strain when I reach the knotted part at the base, and he gives a quick thrust, pushing it inside me. The stretch burns, bringing tears to my eyes, but it feels so good to have him all the way inside me that I let out a helpless groan of pleasure. Axel matches it with one of his own.

"Fuck, Luna," he says, his voice strained. "You feel so fucking good."

He thrusts harder, my back slamming against the tree. I think again of Ama watching, and my core throbs with heat. Axel lowers his head to my neck again and bites me viciously as he pumps into me. My own wolf tears toward the surface, and I let her claws out, raking them through his skin, inhaling the intoxicating scent of our mate's blood and sweat. I spread my legs as wide as I can, lolling my head to the side so he can savage my entire neck if he wants to. He can rip my throat out, I don't care, as long as he keeps fucking me.

His tongue slides along my throat, lapping at the blood, and I rake my claws through his flesh again, slamming my hips against his and crying out each time he rams his cock into me. The knot has grown so big he can hardly move, stretching me until I'm panting and begging for more in the same breath I beg him to stop, it's too much. My wolf pushes closer to the surface, and I bite down on his shoulder as his cock swells further still, tearing a shriek from my throat. I wrap my legs around him and ride up and down, but I can't pull free of his swollen knot.

I throw my head back and scream as he pumps deep into my core. I'm swimming in searing pain and ecstasy. I can't tell which is more severe. And with someone watching us from the woods and Axel's teeth clamped to my skin, I erupt in an orgasm so intense it threatens to tear me to pieces. My spirit shoots off into the sky from the intensity of pleasure coursing through me. I scream again and again.

Axel throws back his head and roars, claws extending from his hands that grip my hips, holding me down while he grinds deep inside me. Hot spurts of cum shoot into me, filling the core of me as I shriek and writhe and tear at him with fang and claw, a wild thing trapped by the knot stretching me until I can't bear it as he claims me to the depths of my soul. At last, I can't take it another moment, and blackness takes me.

# Chapter Seven

*Luna*

When my eyes flutter open, I'm lying on the ground. Axel is kneeling over me. He slips a couple fingers into me before drawing them out and rubbing the musky-smelling cream into the gashes his teeth left in my neck. My wolf growls with pleasure though it burns. He dips his fingers in me again, then rubs it into the wounds I left on his own shoulders.

"What are you doing?" I demand, sitting up and closing my knees.

"It's a mating practice," he says.

"What is that?" I ask, looking down as more of the stuff trickles out of me, running down my thighs.

"It's my seed," he says. "You can rub it into your cuts to bond with me. You can rub yours into mine, too."

"What kind of seeds?" I ask, narrowing my eyes.

"Wolf seed," he says. "When we mate during your heat, that's what will make the baby grow inside you."

"I don't want your baby inside me," I say, wiping the stuff off my thighs. I sniff my fingers, and my wolf nearly swoons with pleasure. I had extra liquid after I mated with Warrick, but I went to the bathroom, and it came out pretty fast. And it didn't smell like this, like desire itself, like a male's dominance that makes me want to throw myself on the ground and open my legs and beg for more. I narrow my eyes at Axel, waiting for his explanation.

"You're not in heat, so it won't happen," Axel says.

"Why didn't you have seeds before?" I ask.

"I never came before," he says.

"Never?" I ask.

"Not with you," he says.

We stare at each other a long minute. "What does that mean?" I ask.

"It means... I finished," he says. "I climaxed. Like you do every time."

"You mean the thing you said you wouldn't do, because it was only for my pleasure?"

He purses his lips. "Yes," he grits out at last. "Do you expect me to fuck you to orgasm every time, and then you leave me wanting?"

"You promised me you wouldn't take your own pleasure with me," I say, glaring at him.

"So this is my punishment?" he asks. "Fucking you until I feel you come all over my cock, your tight cunt pulsing around me, and I'm not allowed to orgasm? Fuck that, Luna. I'm going to come inside you, and I'm going to keep coming inside you until you're stuffed full of my babies. And every time you have one, I'm going to fill you with another one until we have a hundred pups underfoot. I'm going to love every single one of them because they're *our* babies, because they show you how much I love you and want you and want to be your mate. And we're going to raise them to be strong, proud, brave wolves instead of teaching them to be afraid of their own shadow and everyone else."

"Are you talking about Mama?" I ask, my eyes narrowing with fury. Before he can answer, I whirl and stomp off through the underbrush.

"Where are you going?" he says, rushing by my side.

"To the fucking truck. Our hunting game is finished, don't you think?" As I storm through the marshland, we pass the carcass of the Key deer we caught and killed. I don't want to remember that moment—I don't even want to think about how fun it was to hunt by Axel's side, working together to bring down our prey. I let out a growl of exasperation and quicken my pace.

Axel stalks beside me. His expression is as dark as the clouds overhead. We continue to power forward, silent save for the rumble of thunder that ripples through the sky. When we get to the truck, Axel lifts me onto the seat. "You want my cum out of you?" he demands.

Without waiting for an answer, he pushes me flat on the seat and dives between my legs, sucking and fucking me with his tongue until all the fight is drained from me, and in its place is the pleasure he keeps drowning me with until I forget what's real. I can't stop myself, though. I come hard again, whimpering and trembling as my walls clench around his long, skillful tongue.

When he's done, we dress, and then he buckles me in and climbs in the driver's seat. He doesn't say a word all the way home, and neither do I. Fury and frustration pours from his body in waves—he doesn't need words to convey how he's feeling. My wolf can feel it.

Rain spatters the windshield as he speeds through the soggy streets, and his wipers sluice the water back and forth. It's not a fierce storm, not yet. It's only a preview of what's to come if it blows in off the ocean. I've lived through the same storms as the civilized world, only in the untamed wilderness of Bogbeast Waters, and I know them well.

Axel parks the truck outside his house, exits the driver's side, and strides around the front bumper to open my door for me. I don't need his help. I don't want him to erase my anger again, to make me feel good when I want to keep hating him. I push past him and stalk toward his stupid little house. The whole city of Jacksonville can fall into the sea for all I care.

I intend to head straight to my bedroom and lock the door, but I halt when I see Ama lounging on Axel's couch as usual. She's watching the television like she lives here, and an angry feeling rises in me, a feeling like she shouldn't be here even if I'm not. I shouldn't care. I've been living away from Axel, connecting with three other men. But the thought of him connecting with her that way makes me want to rip out her entrails like we did the Key deer.

Ama bolts to her feet, sniffing the air and glowering like she's picturing our entrails, too. "You fucked, didn't you?"

"None of your fucking business," Axel snaps from behind me. "Get out of my house."

A pout forms on Ama's pretty face, and her chin quivers. "I knew it."

Axel only points toward the screen door we just entered. "Out."

She folds her arms over her small breasts and stands her ground. "I can smell it on the two of you. You had sex. I know what your cum smells like."

Axel grinds his teeth and glares. "What I do or don't do with Luna is none of your business, Ama. You're my Second, not my mother."

"You mean, not your *mate*," she snaps.

"That, too," he says coldly. "Now leave before I lose my temper."

Though Axel only uses words and not his dominance display—I notice he almost never uses that—Ama stomps across the room and out the front door. A smug little seed of happiness sprouts in my belly. He defended me, picked me over her. I don't want him, but I also don't want her to have him. I just don't like her, and she doesn't deserve the kind of pleasure he gives me.

When she's gone, a wave of relief like a thorn plucked from my paw passes through me.

"Get cleaned up," Axel says. "I'll make us a drink, and we can talk."

I gawk at him, blinking. He's speaking calmly like we haven't been fighting or fucking all day. "What if I don't want to?"

"Do it anyway," he says before striding into the kitchen like he doesn't have the energy for my defiance right now. I'm not sure which of us will wear the other down first.

I obey him, just like Ama did, though. As I stand beneath the warm spray of water, I wonder how he gets us to do his bidding without involving his wolf. Does he get Ama to do things by making her feel as good as me? And why does she know what his explosion smells like? Does he do that with her, too? If she makes him feel as good as he makes me when I explode, why isn't he with her?

He must know that there's something better—me. Just like I know that no matter how good he makes my body feel, I want someone else, too.

But until I can escape, I'll just have to see what exactly Axel is planning. When I'm clean, dry, and dressed, I head out to the kitchen.

Axel looks up from his seat at the table. A tray of smoked and dried meat and cheeses rests in front of him, along with two uncapped beers in frosted bottles. His hair is damp, and it hangs in soft curls at his neck. He's wearing jeans and a skin-tight t-shirt that shows off his rippling muscles. Before I can stop my thoughts, my wolf pushes forward with pride and admiration at the strong, commanding presence of our Alpha.

*No, not our Alpha,* I remind her. *Warrick is our Alpha.*

*Our mate, then,* she argues. But he's not our mate, either. He's our captor.

"Have a seat," Axel says. "I want to talk to you about pack law. As the Alpha and his mate, we're part of a larger family—the Jacksonville pack. And that pack is part of an even bigger family—the southeast territory. Then there's the United States, and beyond that, the werewolf race as a whole. There are packs all around the world. Each of those levels within the hierarchy has rules and structures to maintain."

I take a drink of beer, thinking of the triplets and how much simpler their life is. All these explanations are making my head spin. "Won't they be mad if they find out I'm your mate again? You said they'd never accept me since I talked to the vampires about y'all."

"Once you're my mate, we'll explain to the pack why it was worth it to give up part of our territory. Together we'll be the most powerful leaders in the southeast, and our pack will be stronger and more respected as well. They won't question it."

"Except for Ama," I say. "She'll question everything."

A scowl flits across his face, but he continues. "That's her right as my Second," he says. "And to be fair, her job as well. If I'm not making decisions for the good of the pack, she has to call me on it. She can even challenge me as Alpha. Besides her, we have warrior wolves who protect the pack in a more physical sense. Our sentinel is Kato. He keeps his eyes and ears open and alerts me of danger to the pack."

"Like me?" I ask. "Am I a danger?"

"Are you?" Axel asks, his eyes searching me with unusual intensity.

"No," I say, setting down my beer. "I don't think so."

"The guardian wolves aren't yet warriors." Axel takes a swig of beer. Neither of us are hungry after the hunt, so the food goes untouched. "They help raise our young. Mothers are supreme majesties in the pack. We always watch out for the mothers, since they continue our species."

"What about lone wolves?" I ask, thinking about Mama. They didn't watch out for her.

"Usually, they're younger, dominant males who either challenge the Alpha and lose, in which case they're automatically cast out of the pack, or who want to start a pack of their own because they're too dominant to take command well." Axel tips back his head and swallows the last of his beer. "Or they take off from another pack for their own reasons and wind up here, wanting to join after realizing the dangers out there for a lone wolf. Watch out for lone wolves, though. They can be feral or overly aggressive if they're dominant and don't have a pack to rule."

I frown at his statement, remembering the scent of a wolf in the woods today where we hunted and later, when we mated. I wonder if that was a lone wolf. And then my thoughts drift in search of Ethan, Callan, and Warrick. They were once part of the Jacksonville pack. Now they choose to live on their own, with only each other to protect. I wonder if that's why Warrick's so grumpy—not enough wolves to lead.

God, how I miss them.

"As the Alpha's mate, you'll have a very important role, too," Axel continues. "You will help me lead and use your practical knowledge and calmer temperament to keep order in the pack. We will truly be victorious when we're together. We can even plan an attack on the bloodsuckers to reclaim our territory. They'll regret ever fucking with us."

Axel squeezes his beer bottle so hard I think it might shatter in his hands. I can practically see the steam billowing from his ears.

"So, would I be a warrior or guardian?" I ask. "Or a mother?"

"You're a submissive wolf," he says. "That doesn't mean you're any less important than the most dominant

Alpha. In fact, a pack can't exist without submissives. Too much dominant energy, and we'd all be fighting and tearing apart each other and the pack. A submissive is a peacekeeper, the glue that holds the pack together and the grease that keeps it running smoothly. The dominant's first job is to protect the submissives. My most important job is to protect you, because you'll be the highest-ranking member of the pack aside from me."

"Oh," I say slowly. "So that's why Ama doesn't like me."

Axel looks at me a long moment. "Sure," he says at last, though his tone makes it clear I'm missing something.

"And because she wants you for a mate," I say.

He picks at the corners of the label with his short fingernails. "Also, I don't know if you know this, but all pack members live in this neighborhood. It runs up to the edge of the preserve. It's part of our territory."

I notice that he didn't answer the question about Ama, but I know I'm right. After a while, Axel goes out to take care of pack business, but I see Ama on the porch swing, so I know I'm still being guarded. I watch TV until I fall asleep on the couch. When I wake, it's dark outside the windows, and Axel is lifting me into his arms.

I let him carry me upstairs, cradling me against his muscular chest, and deliver me to my bedroom. There, he straightens the wrinkled blue sheets he covered the bed with and lays me down on the soft mattress, where he proceeds to strip me bare.

I burrow my head into my pillow, ready to slip back into the land of dreams. But Axel has different ideas. He climbs on the bed with me and pulls me into his arms.

"I can't get enough of you, Luna," he murmurs into my lilac hair. "I'm a man possessed."

He begins to kiss my ear, and shivers of pleasure move through me in waves. I lie back, languid and sleepy, while he kisses down my neck. After a while, he scoots down, his fingers skimming over my skin, making goosebumps rise. When his mouth lands on my nipple, sucking and tonguing me, my body comes alive and wetness blooms between my legs. He groans and sucks harder, his fingers teasing as they inch lower. He moves to the other nipple, leaving the first one red and erect, glistening with his saliva.

His hands move over me, stroking and caressing. Then he moves his mouth across my skin, nipping and licking my neck, kissing my mouth, and nibbling my ear lobe. Yet again, I'm on fire, thrumming with a connection that goes far deeper than I like. After a while, he works his way down my body and settles my legs. His tongue torments me into a frenzy. He's aroused, too, as evidenced by his rigid shaft, but he does nothing to satisfy himself. This is for me, like he promised before, but I find myself wishing it wasn't, because I want that deep pounding of his cock that he gave me earlier.

When I explode around his fingers in orgasm, he hums into my pussy. It's a hum of satisfaction at making me come so quickly. He doesn't stop, though. He replaces his fingers with his tongue, pushing it inside me and working his fingers over the little bud of pleasure until I explode again. When he's finally had enough, he lays beside me, nuzzling my neck.

"Your satisfaction is my satisfaction, Luna. I'll save my orgasms until you forgive me."

He falls asleep next to me, but I can't rest easy. I swear I can hear the triplets howling for me in the back of my mind. Longing rips through my heart, tearing me to pieces. I have to go back, to be with the men I love. I'll never be happy without my three biker lovers. They're my family, no matter what Axel says.

As soon as Axel's breathing deepens and his lips softly part, I remove his hand from my belly and slide away from him. I pause, looking at this man who gives me so much pleasure and so many promises. I feel for him, but I don't belong here.

I dress, tiptoe into the hallway, and make my way downstairs. My heart swells in my chest as I step outside and breathe in the night. It's time to go home.

# Chapter Eight

*Ethan*

I've been hunting in the swamp all evening when I catch the scent of something so potent, so mind-blowingly powerful, I practically trip over my own feet. I smell Luna, as sure as the day is long. Excitement thrums through my veins, and I take off at breakneck speed, my paws splashing through the mud and sand. We haven't seen hide nor hair of our woman since the vampires attacked and made off with her.

I bolt through the underbrush, tearing over the land, not thinking about anything but Luna. Not thinking that she's not our woman but Warrick's woman. As far as I'm concerned, she belongs to all of us, even if she's the first woman I've ever wanted that I won't get to fuck. I don't even think about what will happen if this is a trap. I'm ready to rip apart any vamps who stand in my way. I fucking dare them to try to stop me from getting Luna back.

At last, I come upon a collapsed structure on a tiny hillock of land in the bog. There's no sign of our pup. It smells of mold and decay, but even that can't erase the sweet scent of our Luna. Certain she must be around here somewhere, I race to the north, the east, the south, and the west but find nothing. Crushed, I drag my ass back to sit before her destroyed dwelling.

Damned if I don't miss her like a motherfucker. I've barely slept since she's been gone. Instead, I lay in the dark, tossing and turning, remembering the short time that she was in our presence and thinking about shit I should've done different.

I've never felt this way about a woman before, and it fucks with my head. In my world, women are a means to an end. And the end usually lands eight inches deep inside them. But none of that was half as satisfying as the brief encounters with the little purple-haired she-wolf who came into our lives and turned us all upside down. And no other woman ever kept me up at night when I wasn't fucking her.

I'm about to throw back my head and howl when I catch the scent of another wolf. The smell is as familiar as it is unwelcome.

Axel paddles through the water, pulls himself up onto the little island, and shakes himself, spraying water over me. I let out a sharp growl, but instead of fighting, he shifts into human.

"I'm not here to fight," he says.

I narrow my eyes and growl low in my throat. When the bastard makes no move to shift back and fight, I grudgingly shift into human form to communicate.

We have a history with the Jacksonville pack, and that history starts and ends with Axel. After our brutal upbringing, Axel took us in and the pack became our family. It beat living with an angry, drug-addicted father and a mother who was too beaten down to protect us. Life with our parents was shit, and we split at age sixteen and never looked back. Axel and the Jacksonville crew embraced us, and it pisses me off that we owe the motherfucker, even if we'd never admit it.

"Aren't you a little far from your territory?" I taunt. "Shouldn't you be babysitting the vampires who now occupy half of Creebay?"

He frowns. "How do you know that?"

I shrug. "Word gets around."

In truth, the vamps caught us hunting on Creebay land, since we like to hunt on Jacksonville pack's territory to piss off their Alpha. Turns out, that land doesn't belong to them anymore.

"It was worth it," Axel says, as smoothly as if we're shooting the shit over a card game. "To get Luna back."

A growl rises in my throat. He doesn't deserve Luna—not after wrecking their True Mate bond and her lost little wolf pup heart.

"You're the bastard who took Luna?"

"Yeah, that's me," he says. "The bastard who saved her from the silver cage the vampires had her in."

"What?" I demand, rage throbbing in my temple at the thought of Luna being burned that way. A silver burn hurts like nothing else.

"That's right," Axel says. "I gave up half our pack land for her. What did you give up? Nothing, because you have nothing to give."

My fingers clench into fists—in part because he's right.

"I might have hurt her," he admits. "But I realized my mistake, and I'm making amends. I'll spend the rest of my life making it up to her. She's worth it. I'll do whatever it takes to keep her by my side."

"What about what she wants?" I ask.

"She doesn't know what she wants. She hasn't experienced enough to make an informed choice. But we both have." His head cocks to the side, and he fixes me with a squinty-eyed glare. "And we both know what's best for her. I can give her everything a she-wolf needs, and you can't. With me, she'll have the protection of an entire pack, the social customs and companionship of similar wolves. All of her needs will be met—socially, emotionally, physically. What can you provide her?"

I want to rip his fucking head off as he speaks. My breath billows from my lungs at a rapid pace at the realization that he's right. My brothers and I don't need anyone else, but that doesn't mean she doesn't. She's not a rough and ready biker living outside of the law. Luna is sweet and gentle, the type of woman who deserves friends and a good, full life, not the tawdry life we can give her.

I'm too pissed to even speak. Instead, I shift and race away through the swamp, my head hammering with fury. A wolf is a social animal. We need bonding, play, wolves all along the spectrum from submissive to the most dominant Alpha. In truth, we probably need that, too. But we don't fucking have it. For a moment, it felt like we had it all with Luna. We can't keep her from all that Axel's offering, though. She deserves a pack.

We're three strong as fuck dominant males. We might be able to provide her with protection, but all the other stuff—Examples of submissive males, older mothers who can help her with her pups, submissive and dominant females she can learn from... Yeah, we can't compete with that.

My chest is so tight I can't breathe as I tear through the marsh. I've got to get Luna out of my system in the only way I know how—get hammered and hammer some pussy.

It takes me nearly forty minutes to get back home, and when I do, Callan and Warrick are nowhere to be found. I take a quick shower, dress in cleanish Levis and a Henley, and head out to hop on my fully restored Harley motorcycle, circa the mid-2020s. She's a forty-year-old beast of a ride with high-performance capabilities and the loudest, most powerful engine this city has ever seen. If she were any faster, she could parasail across the swamp.

The sky's so dark it blots out the moon and every star. It's going to be a whale of a storm whenever it hits. The wind howls as I power along the driveway, but it matches my angry mood. Once I hit the paved road, I speed along at about one-twenty. Cars and trucks move out of my way as if they can feel my rage.

Other supernaturals in the area hole up at Gideon's Bar when it floods, but my mood's a little rough for that crowd. Instead, I head to the Demon's Eye, a favorite biker bar my brothers and I frequent. I park my bike, swing my leg off the frame, and stride inside.

The bar's dark and dingy, just the way I like it. As I storm across the concrete floor, every patron lifts their head to look at me, no doubt feeling the energy I leave in my wake as I pass their tables or booths. The bartender, a swarthy panther shifter named Dagger, looks up when I stalk toward the steel and carbon bar-top at the back of the pub.

"Y'look like ya need somethin' stiff and strong," he says, grinning with a feral glint in his eyes. Like most of the panthers, he's a First Nations cat. He's got shoulder length black hair tied back with a bandana, and like most people in this bar, he's got scars and tats and missing teeth to show for the crowd he prefers.

"The stiffer, the better," I growl, planting my ass on the bar stool.

"I got jus' whatcha need. How 'bout an Irish Car Bomb? Part Guinness, part whiskey, part Irish-cream—all ready to fuck you up." The gold grill in his mouth glints in the dim light.

"Make it a double, and you've got yourself a deal." I swivel in my seat, eyeing the bar for a fuckable woman. Guilt swells inside me, like I'm cheating on Luna, which is fucking pathetic, since she didn't even choose me when she was with us. Axel is right—we're not equipped to give her a full life. All I'm equipped to do is fuck a woman good and hard, give her a few orgasms to write home about, and send her packing. I shove the thought of Luna roughly away and spy a couple of hotties watching me in return. They look like the kind of women who need nothing more than what I can give—a good, deep dicking.

Dagger slides the glass of dark chocolate-colored liquid in my direction, and I start to lift it to my mouth.

"Not s' fast," Dagger says, reaching for a shot glass filled with a creamy mocha substance. "Wait for the good stuff. Gotta to chug the whole thing before the cream curdles." He chuckles, making the scars on his face and neck dance as he drops the entire shot glass into the Guinness.

"To better times," I say, hefting the mug.

"Better times," he says with a nod, planting his palms on the bar top.

I tip back my head and drain the drink, pushing away the shot glass with my tongue. Then I slam the mug back on the counter. "Hit me up with another."

"Y'got it." Dagger turns and gets busy with my second drink.

The first was only a warm-up...I plan on getting so wasted tonight that all thoughts of Luna are drowned.

Half a dozen Car Bombs later, my mind is starting to fuzz out when a warm hand slides across my back. My first thought is, *Luna!*

When I pivot, there's one of the hotties from across the bar. Even three sheets to the wind, I can tell she's not as pretty as she looked from across the room. Looks won't get me what I crave, though—a good lay who can squeeze Luna right out of my mind.

"Help you?" I growl.

"Is that your best line?" she asks with a teasing smile.

"I don't need a fucking line."

"Well, then it's your lucky day, because you can help me, in fact," she says, swaying on her feet. "You can help me quench this fire." She runs her palm across her body. She's wearing a skin-tight, see-through t-shirt that shows off her black bra.

"Good, then let's go." I slide from the bar stool, grab her hand, and drag her toward the exit.

"No foreplay?" she teases.

"We both know we want to fuck. Let's skip the formalities."

She shrugs and grins at her friend. Her friend should be concerned that she's going off with a man like me, but then, what do I know? She probably does this as much as I do. I haul the woman out the back door into the alley. It stinks of piss and garbage, but I've dropped my share of used condoms in the swill back here.

When we're deep into the shadows, I push her against the bricks and savage her mouth with mine. She tastes like cigarettes and beer, but she's willing and responsive. My dick, however, seems to have a mind of its own—it's not rising to the opportunity.

She grinds her hips against me, and I know she can feel the disappointing show happening in my jeans. Like the whore she is, she drops to a crouch, unzips my fly, and takes my limp dick into her mouth. This'll work—blow jobs always get me off. I can fingerfuck her to make her happy afterwards.

But, no, her mouth and her tongue aren't working, either. I can get it up, but just barely, and I'm nowhere near finishing even after fifteen minutes of her best work. I keep picturing Luna and losing my concentration. I want *her* mouth on me. I want to touch her, to taste her, to hold her. Hell, I want to be with her, near her, even if I never get to fuck her. Just sitting beside her on the porch swing at night, shooting the shit with a few beers, is better than a blowjob from a stranger.

What the fuck is happening to me?

I grab the woman's head and ease her away from me. "Sorry, babe, it ain't happening tonight."

I turn and stomp off down the alley, ghosting the woman who thought she'd scored tonight.

"Hey," she yells. "Limp dick asshole!"

I groan and throw my leg over my bike. If I can't even have a meaningless lay to satisfy my needs, I'm well and truly fucked.

# **Chapter Nine**

*Luna*

I took a wrong turn at a creek in my excitement to see the triplets. Now, morning is coming, damp and chilly from the cloud cover which obscures the stars. Good thing I've got thick fur and sure feet, so I don't fall into the warm swamp water.

As I run, I imagined every reunion the men and I could have when I see them again. I pictured their surprise and delight, their crushing hugs and soft kisses, their passion, and wonder. All of the images in my head are happy ones.

So why do I feel so guilty at leaving Axel?

For one, he wasn't horrid to me—not by a long shot. Not this time. But I don't trust him, and if I don't trust him, how can we be together?

We can't.

Besides, I don't want to be his mate. I want to be with Warrick, Ethan, and Callan.

Right?

I slow my run to a loping pace. Just then, I catch the scent I caught earlier, when I was hunting with Axel. Is whoever was watching me earlier following me now? This thought sends a ripple of fear along my spine. It was exciting when I pictured Ama watching Axel fuck me, overcome with his desire for me. Having her stalk me through the woods and catch me alone? Not so exciting.

I slink into the underbrush and listen intently with my nose tipped up to scent the air, a knot of dread and fear pulling tight in my belly. Now that I have time to really take in the scent, I'm less sure that it's Ama. It smells like... Something familiar. Maybe it's a male's smell. I fought Ama once, and though I don't remember her scent, I don't think this was it. When I don't hear anything, I venture back out into the clearing, intending to make haste toward the triplets' place.

Suddenly, an enormous wolf attacks me, knocking me to the ground. I've never seen a wolf this big—and

I've seen the triplets in wolf form. Axel's words about "watch out for a lone wolf" swim through my mind as the wolf sinks its teeth into me.

I scream piteously, sure this guy will tear me to shreds. I have no chance against a wolf this big. But I have no choice but to fight, so I yelp and wriggle, finally raking my back paw down his belly, where the fur can't protect him. He roars, and I shoot out from under him and run for my life. My mind is whited out with fear, making it impossible to take a full breath or think of a better strategy than to flee. The swamp's ahead, and I race for it, leaping into the water and swimming like mad.

I scramble up the bank to the other side of the water, grateful an alligator didn't have me in his sights, since I'm bleeding bad from where the wolf bit me. Then I race for home. Out of nowhere, the lone wolf rockets from my left and attacks. His knife-like teeth catch purchase on my neck, and he shakes.

I cry out and struggle, howling like a banshee. I kick and claw, trying to break his hold on me, but he's too damn strong. My short life flashes before me, and I know this is the end.

He continues to shred my neck, growling and tightening his jaws.

My consciousness starts to fade. I know I'm losing blood, too much to survive. I'll be dead before I had a chance to really live, outside of the lonely swamp existence with Mama, which was really just surviving. Before I had a chance to really love, to tell the triplets I love them all, and to tell Axel… I don't know what.

Just before my lights go out, I call silently for Warrick, Ethan, Callan, even Axel, begging for them to save me. Then I realize that's all wrong, that I need to tell them how I feel. That they made a difference in my life. That I love the wild motorcycle men who were banished like me, and I wish my rejected mate the best in leading the Jacksonville pack.

Without telling them anything, though, I succumb to death's cold embrace.

# Chapter Ten

*Warrick*

I sit on the porch swing and light up the first cigarette of the day. I'm up before the light because Ethan came stumbling in drunk just before dawn, crashing around like the inconsiderate asshole he is and waking the rest of us. I'm surprised he didn't bring home a woman, but he hasn't done that since Luna came to stay with us.

She's gone now, though. He could bring home a woman. I wouldn't stop him. We need to let her go, all of us. I want my brothers to be happy, and I want Luna to be happy, and this is the best way. I haven't told my brothers, but I know where she is. I crept through the Creebay preserve, watching for signs of her every night since the vamps took her. Surely I'd catch her scent if they let her out.

But I didn't find her around the vampires' lair. I found her in the woods with Axel, hunting and then fucking. At first, I wanted to rip both their throats out. But as the gut-punched sensation drained, and I saw her come hard for him before he rubbed his seed into her marks as a claiming, I realized I couldn't intervene. She was with her mate, and he was satisfying her in every way. If she'd been a simple chosen mate before, not a True Mate, I would have fought for her. But nothing can interfere with a True Mate bond. Obviously, even severing it couldn't unbind their wolves from each other.

We were a bunch of fools to think we could ever be more than a temporary refuge for her battered heart.

I finish my cigarette and flick the butt into a puddle off the side of the porch. It lands with a quick sizzle. I hear something near the edge of the swamp and perk up my ears. From the sound of it, two wolves are in a fight to the death.

And even though I didn't interfere with Luna, she's my first thought. It's one thing to admit she's better off with that prick Axel. A mating bond is sacred, and I want her to be happy, even though I despise that motherfucker and don't think for a second that he deserves her. But she seemed happy as fuck when I saw them together, and if I put my ego aside, I have to admit that the Jacksonville pack can offer her protection and safety in numbers, something me and my outlaw brethren can't.

But if someone so much as lays a paw on her...

I shift and race toward the sound without a moment's hesitation. As I get closer, I smell her, and my pace quickens. I tear through the underbrush to get to her.

*My baby girl, Luna.*

I burst into the clearing just in time to see some asshole wolf ripping out the flesh in Luna's throat. Rage floods through my limbs, and I lunge for the wolf. He's bigger than me, and when I leap at him, he flings me clear across the swamp. I've never known a wolf so strong— not naturally. He must be hopped up on goblin blood or some other artificial enhancement. And he attacked our sweet, gentle, little Luna. In a rage, I fly back at him, fueled by desperation and a fury so deep even his superior size and strength can't stop me. In a blur of fang and claw, I slash and rip until I tear his throat out and then rip his body limb from bloody limb.

Before he's even stopped twitching, I shift back to human and scoop up Luna in my arms. Her body hangs like dead weight, everything drooping toward the earth. I spring into action, setting my legs to sprinting as the life force drains from her body.

I'm not a religious man, but as I race for the house, I pray to all the demons in hell she'll make it out of this alive. Slowly, she begins to shift in my arms, first a leg, then her head, as if she doesn't even have the strength to turn fully human. But finally, as I reach the house, she's back in her human form. Her skin holds a ghostly gray pallor, like the edges of the swamp after a storm, and I'm sure I'm too fucking late.

The second I get within earshot of our house, I start to yell, screaming at the top of my lungs. "Callan, goddamn it! Get something for Luna. She's dying in my arms!"

When I burst into sight of our cabin, my brothers are already in action, racing toward me. Callan's got the medical bag in hand. A medic he ain't, but he knows enough to deal with all our injuries. Ethan's got a stack of towels and rags. As soon as he sees me, he spreads a large towel on the sparse grass in front of our house. "Lay her here. Quick! I'll get whatever Callan needs."

I practically skid onto the ground, scraping the skin off my knees as I gently lie Luna on the towels. She rolls like dead weight onto the ground, and her crimson lifeblood blooms across the cotton fabric.

"What the fuck happened?" Ethan snarls.

"Wolf attack. That motherfucker's gone to his maker in pieces," I growl back.

"Give me your hand, Warrick," Callan commands. "Press here to staunch the flow."

I do as he says, pressing my hand against the artery out of which her blood spurts.

"Harder. Stop the flow," Callan says. "Ethan, go get alcohol and peroxide from the bathroom. I'm going to try to stitch up this artery, then put her neck back together."

He gently picks up the flap of skin that was once attached to her neck and now hangs by a mere half-inch of skin. I'm in no fucking way squeamish, but I about hurl at the sight.

Ethan races into the house, flinging open the screen door so hard it thwaps against the wall before it bangs shut.

"You're doing great, Warrick," Callan mutters, pulling out one of his kits from the medical bag. He can say that, but my heart is thundering inside my ribcage, ready to explode if she dies. One night with her wasn't near enough. A couple months was nothing. I want a whole fucking life of time with her.

"I'm going to wad a clean towel around your hand to staunch the peripheral blood loss," Callan says. He picks out a needle, threading it with whatever he uses to stitch us all up. He's had plenty of opportunities to sew our wounds closed through the years. He's got the needle threaded by the time Ethan bounds out of the house.

"Pour the alcohol all over this needle," Callan says.

Ethan unscrews the bottle and sloshes it onto the needle.

"Gonna try and work around your fat fingers, brother," Callan says to me. "Move a millimeter to the right."

I do as he commands, since Callan is the king of this arena. He pierces the artery and makes his first stitch. "Do you remember how to check her blood pressure, Ethan?"

"Sure," Ethan says, already rummaging through the kit. He lifts the cuff and stethoscope from the bag and moves around to the other side of Luna. He affixes it to her arms, fits the earpieces inside his ears, and puffs up the cuff.

I tune him out, focused on keeping pressure on Luna's artery, until Ethan calls, "Seventy over fifty."

"Shit," Callan says, "She's shocking." His fingers move sure and steady as he stitches the blood vessel closed. Finally, he says, "Okay, we got that to stop. Now, the neck flap. Hold this towel in place, Warrick. Ethan, gauze."

With finesse, he places the skin back in position and starts to stitch. "Run and get some water—room temperature would be good."

"On it," Ethan says, already in motion.

I've lived through hurricanes, vamp attacks, and more bar fights than most men have under their belt in a lifetime. I can handle pain with the calm of a Zen master. But witnessing the damage done to my darling baby girl by that fucking wolf makes me about lose my head. I want to rip that wolf to shreds ten times over, but he's already dead. I can't do a damn thing now except hold a fucking towel.

Ethan rushes back as Callan ties off the last stitch in her neck. As Ethan pours water, Callan twists off the top of the peroxide. When the water is gone, my middle brother empties the peroxide bottle on Luna's neck. "Open a couple of those four by fours and dig for the medical tape in the bottom of my bag."

"Got it," I say, relieved to have a task.

Callan tapes gauze onto the wound before taking a deep breath and sitting back on his haunches. Then, the action finished, we just sit there, staring at each other over Luna's little body.

"She's still breathing," Ethan offers.

"What now?" I ask, irritated at being in a subordinate position to my brother.

"We get her into the house where she'll be warm and dry." Callan glances at the sky with its dark looming clouds. "Then we wait. She'll either make it or she won't, depending on the strength of her wolf."

# Chapter Eleven

*Luna*

I'm stuck in the world between the worlds. I run. I run through bloody marshes teeming with monsters who chase me in endless loops. I race through crimson swamps lined with alligators waiting to consume me if I dare approach the shore. There are infinite dangers, unending treachery waiting for me, and there's no escape, ever.

A trickle of warm water drips onto my skin, and I try to scream and look up, sure that I'll see blood pouring from the Spanish moss hanging above. But a feeble squeak is all that comes from my lips.

"Luna." A gentle, urgent, *familiar* voice calls, and I feel myself being shaken. At long last, my lids flutter open, ending my nightmare.

I blink rapidly, trying to orient myself. I'm in a room, my room. Gentle hands bathe me with a warm cloth. A bearded man sits over me, but when my eyes open, he drops the cloth into a bowl of water and just stares.

"Callan," I say, my voice hoarse from disuse. "Is that really you?"

"Luna," he says, a gentle smile on his lips as he brushes my hair back from my forehead. "Oh, pet. You came back to us. Thank fucking Satan himself. We thought you might not make it." He gives a little relieved laugh and leans down, pressing his lips to my forehead for a long moment.

It hurts to be awake, so I close my eyes again. My body feels like it's been replaced with an old carcass that's been picked over by buzzards for days. I moan and reach up to touch something papery soft covering my neck. "What is this?" I croak, prying my eyes open. "What am I doing here? What happened?"

Callan's large, warm hand smooths my hair away from my cheek and I nuzzle into it. His voice is low and gentle, like a caress. "You were attacked by a rogue wolf in the forest. Warrick found you and brought you home, and I stitched you up."

"A rogue wolf..."

"Don't you remember?" He picks up a soft towel and pats my damp skin.

I scrunch up my face as I strain to remember, but the only thing that comes up is running away from something...or someone...in the woods. And then there's nothing but holes in my mind. "No," I croak. "I was running from someone."

He continues to stroke my hair. "The mind is powerful. It's trying to protect you."

"I'm glad to be home," I murmur. A slight smile lifts the corners of my mouth as I open my eyes to study Callan's beautiful face. "How dead is the wolf?"

"Unrecognizable body parts," Callan says with a chuckle. "Warrick is thorough."

I chuckle, too, until the sound turns into a cough. I roll onto my side and wheeze for a second. I'm happy to be back where I belong, but everything feels strange as well as familiar after so long away. "How long have I been here?"

"You've been out of it for over a week while your wolf healed you from within. One of us has been with you twenty-four seven, protecting you in case..." He retrieves his washrag from the basin of water that sits the small fridge next to the bed. Then he draws it across my back.

"In case what?" I ask, trying not to lose my train of thought and sink into the bliss of being bathed by Callan's strong, rough hands that are so gentle in their care for me. The rough texture of the warm, wet washcloth is a spring-day-in-the-sun at Bogbeast Waters kind of feeling.

"The wolf is dead, but we don't know where it came from or who sent it," Callan says. "Or why it attacked."

I don't want to think about that. All I want to think about is how good it feels when he continues to dip the cloth in the basin, wring it out, and cleanse my body. When he's done, he pats my skin dry. Then his hands swish together and land on my back with something like a liquid silk sensation.

"Oh!" I say, my eyelids fluttering open. "What's that?"

"It's oil," he says. "To keep your skin smooth. But I can massage you if you like it."

"I do," I say, my voice half-moan. "Keep going." I close my eyes, and after about ten minutes, I roll onto my back so he can get at my front.

He scoots to the bottom of the bed, and his hands glide across my feet and legs, massaging and caressing. The sensation is divine. His slick palms travel up to my hips, belly, and breasts. His fingers twirl and tweak my nipples, stirring my heat into a frothing pool of want. No one has ever touched me this way, and I never want it to stop.

I writhe into his tender but firm touch. What mere tenderness a few minutes ago becomes a torment, teasing my desire awake. I open my eyes and find him studying me intently as he caresses my skin. "Oh, Callan... It feels so good."

"Yeah?" he says, swallowing hard.

"Yeah," I breathe, widening my legs, hoping he'll massage between them.

He hisses in a breath as his fingers slide between my legs, answering my unspoken plea. He rubs gently through my folds, slickening them even more with the silky oil. At last, he slowly pushes a finger inside me. We both suck in a breath at once.

"Can you take off your clothes, too?" I ask. Last time, when we were in the kitchen, I didn't know what this fire in my belly meant. Now, thanks to Axel, I know how to get the relief I need.

"Luna…" Callan begins.

"What?" I ask.

He draws his hand from between my legs and starts massaging my thighs again, which only makes my craving grow. "The last night you were here, you chose Warrick."

"And today I choose you," I say, lifting my hips, urging him to return to the heat throbbing between my legs.

"That's not how it works," he says, shaking his head.

"Why not?" I ask.

"I don't know," he says. "It just doesn't. Werewolves have one mate."

"I had a mate, and then I had another," I say. "And now I want you to mate with me."

"So, you don't want Warrick anymore?"

"I want him sometimes," I say. "And sometimes I want you. And sometimes maybe I'll want Ethan. You said I had to choose. You didn't say it was forever."

"You want us all to fuck you?" he asks, swallowing so the little lump in his throat bobs.

I whimper, so wet with desire that I can feel it soaking into the bed under me. "Yes," I manage.

Callan slides his fingers between my legs again, pushing two inside me. He strokes across my little nub, and I explode with pleasure. When I'm done clenching around his fingers, he leans down and takes a deep sniff between my legs. "Still want me to fuck you?" he asks with a crooked smile.

"Yes," I moan.

He quickly strips off his clothes and climbs on the bed, stretching the length of his body next to mine. He starts massaging my hip, pushing his stiff cock against my thigh.

"Closer," I breathe. "I need your weight on top of me."

I feel at once aroused and vulnerable, like I might cry one minute and come the next. It's an odd feeling, one that's no doubt the result of nearly losing my life.

"What's the matter, pet?" Callan says, his eyes boring into me with concern, as if he can sense my conflict.

"I don't know," I say, as tears leak out the corners of my eyes. "Just... Hold onto me, and never let me go."

"Never," Callan promises, pulling me into his arms and squeezing me tight against him. "Never again."

"Get on top," I say.

Once he's on top of me, I breathe a sigh of relief. He's warm and heavy, and I feel completely safe under him, like his body is a shield protecting me. He kisses me gently, his soft beard rubbing against my cheeks.

Snug between my hips, he pushes up on his forearms to look down at me. "What do you want, pet? Want me to hold you like this? Whatever you want, I'm here to provide it."

I shake my head, spilling out a few more tears.

"Do you want me to fuck you?"

I nod my head. "Please."

"Okay. But you tell me if anything hurts, okay? I'm not as big as Warrick, but I'm still too big for a lot of women." The intense caring pouring for his gaze is like a balm to my soul.

I sniff in a shuddering breath. "Please," I whisper. "I want you inside me, Callan. You won't hurt me. I want all of you."

He presses his lips to mine and reaches down, fitting the engorged head of his cock inside the opening to my sex. I moan in pleasure at the stretched sensation.

"You like that, don't you, pet?" he asks with a knowing smile.

I nod eagerly and buck my hips under him, trying to impale myself on his cock.

The tip of his tongue lands on his upper lip as he eases his length inside of me, his eyes hooded as he watches my lids widen and my teeth bite down on my lip at the unbearable, delicious ache of his size inside me.

"Need to tap out?" he asks, a smirk on his lips.

"I don't know what that means," I admit, my breath coming short. "But I don't want you out of me."

He chuckles, draws his cock out, and then plunges back in—hard.

I squeak, and he grins like a wolf that just got a fresh kill and laid it out for the approval of his Alpha. It's a gloating smile, one I'm not used to seeing on Callan's face. I like this side of him. "How about now?" he asks. "Am I too much for you, little pet?"

There's a challenge in his voice, like he wants me to give up. "No," I cry, gripping his shoulders to keep him from pulling away.

"You're fucking tight, aren't you, pet?" he asks. "I'll just be here waiting for you to get used to me."

He doesn't move until I start moaning and grinding up against him, scratching at his shoulders to get him going. "Fuck me," I beg. "I've been gone so long. All I wanted was to get back to you and your brothers."

"So we could fuck you?" he asks, sliding out and slamming deep into me again, making tears blur my vision.

"Yes," I moan, rocking my hips up and down.

He lowers himself to his forearms and works himself around and around inside me. A low moan leaves his lips. "Fuck, you feel so good, Luna. I didn't know a pussy could be this tight."

I let out a whimper of pleasure, unable to look away from his eyes that captivate mine and hold me like I'm safe and warm at home. He pulls almost all the way out then drives his cock deep inside me. I eagerly tip my hips up to greet him.

"I'm going to make you come so hard, pet," he growls, setting up a slow, steady rhythm of retreating and thrusting into me so deep I slide up the bed a bit each time our hips meet.

I match him thrust for thrust, panting and scratching his back, pulling him closer, begging for more. The whole time he looks deeply into my eyes, watching my blissful torment unfold. As I gaze back into his eyes, an intense connection forms between us, burning through me, getting me hotter and hotter.

"I'm going to explode," I cry at last, unable to hold myself back.

"Let me feel you come all over my cock, pet," he growls, grinding deep so his pelvic bone smashes against my clit. "Let me feel that pussy milking me."

Words desert me as an explosion of pleasure rocks through me. I cry his name, bucking wildly, my wolf howling inside me.

"Oh, fuck, Luna, here I come," he shouts, and his hips move faster and harder. His head falls back, and he lets out deep grunts and moans as his liquid fire pours into me, sating my core and my wolf's heart.

Our bodies fuse together, and for a minute, I can't do anything but feel the mind-bending bliss and love pouring through us both. Our wolf spirits seem to be dancing together, crashing into, under, around, and through one another. A song I've never heard sings through my soul, like it's fusing with his just as my body has.

When we finally come down, it's this slow, sweet melting, like we're two feathers floating back to earth. At last, Callan slides off me so I can breathe but wraps his arms around me and threads his legs through mine.

"Fuck, that was incredible," he says, a deep sigh of satisfaction heaving through his muscular, tattooed chest. At this moment, I don't care that running back here almost cost my life. As long as I'm with the triplets, I'll die a happy wolf.

# **Chapter Twelve**

*Luna*

My heart is full and my wolf satisfied after Callan's fucking. Cuddling up together, we settle down for a sweet nap. When we wake up, we wrestle in his bed, pinning each other to the mattress with the loser having to deliver kisses to the victor before being released to try again. I can't remember laughing and having so much fun in my life.

Our fun is cut short when a voice bellows outside the house.

"Fucking hell," Callan mutters. "Wait here." He rolls from the bed, yanks on his pants, and heads out of the room.

"No way," I say, scrambling into my clothes. "This is my fault."

I race after him, heading through this house that I love. I glance right and left and notice it's gone backward in the cleanliness department—but not as bad as it was when I first arrived. There are hardly any beer bottles or cans on the floor and only one or two pieces of clothing.

"Luna!" the voice bellows again.

I halt in my tracks. When I heard the call the first time, I thought it was one of Callan's brothers returning and somehow knowing that we'd mated. I remember all the jealousy and conflict I stirred up before. But it's not one of them—my wolf knows.

As happy as she was playing with Callan on the bed, she positively sings inside me as she demands we answer the call of her mate.

But Axel isn't *my* mate, even if our wolves are still bound.

"Luna, I know you're here," he calls. "I can smell you."

The plaintive note in his voice twists a wicked knife of guilt into my heart. How can this be? I'm with the guys I want to be with. But the whispers in my heart tell a different story—they remind me that, in my soul of souls, Axel is my Alpha. My wolf still wants him to be our everything.

Shoving those feelings aside, I barrel outside, determined to put Axel in his place. It must have rained while I was out. The air smells damp and dank as if the gators have wrestled in the swamp, stirring up the swamp gasses.

I skid to a stop on the porch. Axel isn't alone. Callan and Ethan have his arms pinned to his side, and Warrick is watching with his arms crossed over his bare chest and a scowl on his face. All sorts of flutters stir in my chest at the sight of the triplets. But these elated thoughts are crushed by the presence of Axel, writhing and struggling against their grip.

Though the brothers are bigger, Axel's strong, too, and it looks like he might just get free of the hold Callan and Ethan have on him. I chew at my lip, looking from one to another. All these men are fighting for *me.*

It's a far cry from when Axel dragged me from the swamp, then tossed me back like fish guts, making me think no one would ever want me.

The triplets, though, they always treated me right.

"Of course I'm here," I say, crossing my arms and staring back at him defiantly. "I told you I wanted to be with these men. You'd have to be dumber than an demonling not to figure out where I'd gone off to."

Axel glares at me. "Come home, Luna."

"I am home," I say. "Where else would I be? The question is, why are *you* here?"

"To bring you home," he says. "To *our* home. I'll do whatever it takes, Luna. I'll fight to the death to get you back if that's what you want."

"Where was your protection when she needed it?" Warrick demands. "Can't you see her neck? I found her at the brink of death."

Axel stills, and the color drains from his face. "Luna... What happened?"

"A lone wolf tore out her throat," Callan says. "I stitched her together. My brothers and I saved her life."

His chest puffs, and I give him a grateful smile, as proud of him as he seems to be of himself.

"I'm deeply indebted to you," Axel grits out. "But if Luna hadn't run away, she wouldn't have put herself in danger. How could I protect her if I didn't know where she was?"

He directs his gaze at me, his eyes the color of the sky on a winter's afternoon and so full of hurt and accusation that my wolf cowers inside me, shrinking onto her belly to have displeased her Alpha. He's right. If I hadn't run away, I wouldn't have been attacked. It was a stroke of luck that Warrick found me. If not for him, I'd be dead right now.

Warrick, standing tall like an imposing statue, looks as formidable as a bog beast. "She ran away because she doesn't want to be with you," he growls at Axel. "It ain't that complicated."

Axel begins to struggle again. "Luna, tell them that's not true. How we're mending the rifts between us. Tell them what a good time we had hunting and… The other things, too."

"You mean when you fucked and fought like enemies," Warrick says, spitting into the dust near his feet.

Axel's face darkens with fury. "How the fuck do you know that?"

"I was watching you," Warrick says coolly.

"What the fuck is wrong with you?" Axel snarls back. "She's my mate. Stop interfering."

"If she's your mate, why is it that even after you tried to pacify her with a few orgasms, she came right back here?" Warrick taunts. "I'll tell you why. Luna needs a real man wrecking that pussy every night... Three of them, in fact."

With a roar of rage, Axel rips his arm free and clocks Ethan in the jaw. Ethan instantly lays into Axel, landing a powerful blow against Axel's cheek. Blood spurts from Axel's mouth as he shoves Ethan to the ground. He falls on him and starts pounding him with his fists.

I let out a scream—I don't want anything to happen to Axel *or* Ethan.

"Keep Luna safe!" Warrick bellows, heading for the two men jostling on the ground as Callan leaps to my side. He tries to tug me away, but I wrestle out of his grasp.

"Luna, stop!" He whips me around and pins both of my wrists behind my back.

"Quit trying to stop me," I yell, kicking at his shins. "Let me go!"

"Cool your jets," he growls. "This isn't just about you—at least not entirely. It's been a long time coming. This fight's been brewing for years."

Warrick is now straddling Axel and pummeling him with his fists. I can barely see Axel's face through the blood.

Ethan is on his feet again, delivering vicious kicks to Axel with his steel-toed boots. "You mangy motherfucker," he snaps, huffing his breaths out between the barrage of blows. "That's the last time you'll deck me."

Axel draws wolf strength from somewhere and manages to roll Warrick from his belly. Swiftly, he scrambles behind Warrick, lands on his back, positions his hands around Warrick's head, and twists.

Warrick roars and clambers to his feet with Axel still clinging to his shoulders. He backs into a tree and slams Axel into the trunk. Axel lets out a bellow and falls from Warrick's back, rolling across the dirt, barely conscious. Ethan grabs his enemy and hauls him to his feet.

"Have at him, Warrick," he yells. "He's your kill!"

Warrick grins wide enough to show a missing molar and punches the palm of his left hand with his right fist. "Oh, I've been waiting for this for a long time, Golden Boy. Ready to meet your maker?"

He hauls back his arm to send Axel to the wolf pack in the stars with one final blow. I know he can do it. I've seen Warrick in action.

"No!" I scream, twisting out of Callan's grasp and racing toward Warrick.

Warrick's head whips toward me, and he stares in confusion.

I lunge and grab Warrick's beefy bicep. "Don't kill him," I cry. "I'll never forgive you."

Axel's hanging on by spiderwebs at this point. His head lolls on his chest, and Ethan's grip is the only thing keeping him upright.

"You'll never forgive me?" Warrick asks in disbelief. "Why would you want to save a man who severed your mate bond?"

"I don't know," I wail. "Just… Don't do it."

Ethan lets Axel fall. His body slumps onto the ground like a bag of crabs.

I fall to my knees, the sand and dirt grinding into my skin. My hands flutter over Axel's body, smoothing away the bloody hair from his face, patting his swollen jaw.

Warrick and Ethan stand over me as Callan joins them, surrounding me.

"What the fuck is going on here, pet?" Callan says. "You said you wanted to be with us."

"I do," I say. I shake my head, trying to clear the panic and horror at seeing my men's barbaric side. "But I don't want anyone to die because of me. Y'all make your point with fists, and that's just how you are. I accept that.

But you need to accept that I make mine with words. I can make Axel listen to me. He's no good dead."

The triplets exchange a look. "What use is he to us alive?" Ethan asks.

"I don't know," I say. "Guess we'll find out."

# **Chapter Thirteen**

*Luna*

If anything is a testament to the triplets' regard for me, the next few minutes prove it.

"We've got to get Axel into the house to care for his wounds," I say, rising to stand, knowing full well their resistance to having anything to do with Axel.

"Fuck that," Ethan says, crossing his muscular arms over his chest as if to hold himself back from launching into Axel again.

Warrick clamps a hand on Ethan's shoulder. "If my baby girl wants to negotiate with the Alpha of the Jacksonville pack, let her have her way."

"Yeah," Callan says, giving Axel a disgusted look. "He's obviously dick-whipped as fuck if he'd show up here without backup, just asking for us to stomp a mudhole in him."

A slow grin forms on Ethan's bloody lips. "I hadn't thought of that," he says. "But damn, Luna. You sure do have a point. I bet he'd give up his entire pack for one more taste of that sweet little pussy you got him hooked on."

"No fucking way," Warrick snarls. "I let him have her when I thought it was her choice. But she came back here, which means she chose us. No one touches my baby girl without going through me."

I glance at Callan. With all the blood and dust and swamp smells, they must not have noticed that we mated earlier. "We'll help her speak her piece with this mutt," Callan says, spitting on Axel's body. "But Luna's pussy is ours."

I like being called their queen and being told I'm theirs. My wolf preens with joy at his words, even though I know we have a hard conversation ahead. I didn't know Warrick thought if I mated with him that meant I'd be mated to him forever, and I need to correct that misunderstanding. But first, I need to make sure Axel lives.

Callan and Ethan haul him up and carry him into the house, his feet dragging on the ground and his head lolling. I can't tell if he's lost consciousness entirely. They lay him on the couch, and I kneel beside him.

"Get me something to wash away the blood," I say.

Callan retreats to get what I asked for while Ethan and Warrick stand like two giant Seminoles.

When Callan returns with a plastic basin full of water, I reach for the washrag floating inside. After squeezing it out, I gently swipe the blood from Axel's bruised face.

One eye is swollen shut, ringed by two angry gashes, and his lip looks like it's been stung by hornets. I peel up his crimson-stained t-shirt to get at his torso, but Callan stops me and shows me the sharp-edged tool in his hand.

"Scissors," he says, using his thumb and finger to snip at the air. "Cut the damn thing off." He demonstrates this by slicing through the bottom of the shirt. After placing the scissors in my hand, he backs away to stand with his brothers.

Tentatively, I snip at the stained cotton until I get the hang of it. Then, I slice through the whole thing. I place the scissors on the floor and gently smooth away all the fabric from my former mate's discolored chest. Large purple bruises mar his chest and abdomen and ribs, while scrapes and abrasions cover his neck and collarbones. But once all the blood has been cleared away, I can see Axel beneath all the discoloration and swelling.

My heart wars with itself—I care about Axel despite myself, but when I think of our True Mate bond severing, I still hate him, too. In his condition, Axel's busted up face and body reflect what I feel inside.

His good eye opens, and he regards me somberly. "Luna," he manages to say with effort.

"Stop," I say, putting my palm in front of his face. "Let me talk. I don't want none of this fighting between you and the triplets. I get that you hate each other, but you brought this on yourself, Axel. None of this would have happened if you hadn't gone and destroyed our bond. I wouldn't even be with the triplets at all, let alone almost killed, and them almost killing you, and you losing the pack land. I'd still be sad about Mama, but none of the rest would've happened at all. I'd still be yours and yours alone, but you chose a different path." I roll my lips between my teeth to keep from letting out a little hiccup of tears.

"And I'll regret my actions every day of my life," Axel rasps. "But if I have to suffer, even if I have to die to prove how much you mean to me, I'll do it. Just give me a chance to."

The room grows as quiet as a moonless night, and Axel's gaze rises to Warrick. My breath catches in the back of my throat.

"Everything I did, I did it for the good of the pack," Axel continues. "But I'd give up the pack and let Warrick take over just to get you back."

Warrick lets out a grunt from his sentinel stance by the door.

Axel lifts his bruised hand and brushes my hair back from my face. Then, he fingers the gauze bandage at my neck, and a shattered look replaces the tenderness. "If you didn't make it…"

His voice trails off, and he brushes a hand down my arm. I close my eyes, savoring the touch while gathering my thoughts. Finally, I open my eyes.

"Maybe it all had to go down this way," I say.

Axel's scraped-up forehead bunches in a frown. "What do you mean?"

"How else would I have met these men?" I ask. "My heart belongs to them, Axel. Even though my wolf and my body feel good with you, my heart is still busted up where you broke it."

Axel's scowl deepens, but he stays quiet.

I wipe away some blood that's seeped from one of the gashes on his face. "Maybe if you can understand how much these men mean to me, and that they're not going anywhere... If you can accept that they're part of my life and they're my mates now, then I can start to forgive you for severing our True Mate's bond."

A dark storm forms on his face, and he squeezes his eyes shut. When he opens them, his anguish is clear in his gaze. "That's not how it works, Luna. It's against the laws of nature. A wolf has one mate. She is his everything, as he is hers."

I swallow hard. "In this house, we break the law."

This time the silence that fills the air is brittle and hard, like glass with spidery little cracks.

Axel closes his eyes and takes a few deep breaths, with his lips pressed tightly together. "What do you want?" he finally says, opening his eyes.

I take a long, deep breath before answering. "I want to join the pack," I say. "But not as your mate. I want to live in safety on pack land, not to be scared I'll be attacked in the woods. I want my own house on Golden Glade Street, like the other pack members. The triplets can come and go from my house as they please and stay there as much as I want them to. And they get to hunt on Creebay preserve without having to skulk around like criminals."

Axel's jaw juts out in the way it does before he explodes. A look of outrage replaces the anguish in his eyes. "I can't do that," he says, the words sounding forced.

"Then I can't forgive you, and I'll continue to live here," I say, raising my chin.

Axel drags a hand over his face, wincing at the pain he's no doubt causing by touching his battered skin. "You don't know what you're asking."

"I know full well what I'm asking," I snap. "I'm asking you to give me something *I* want, rather than assuming you know what's best for me. Yes, I liked all the mating things we did, but you can't control me by making me feel good. That's not everything a girl wants, Axel."

"Fuck, Luna," Axel says, squeezing his head. Slowly, as if he's aged fifty years, he hauls his body upright. "That's not why…"

"Then think about it like this," I say, as confidence grows at my certainty that I've found just the way to convince him. "A lone wolf attacked me. Remember when you said they could be dangerous? Well, there could be more out there. It could happen again. And maybe next time, Warrick won't be around to save me."

Axel pulls his hair and lets out a low, rumbling groan.

"You said you'd do anything for me," I remind him. "So, prove it. Prove that you mean what you say, and you're not just trying to get me back the way that suits you. Then I'll think about it—after you prove you want *me* to be happy."

Axel flashes the triplets a glare that would incinerate most werewolves. But not my men. My men are stronger and fiercer and scarier than any wolf in the world, I just know it.

"Come on, Axel," I say. "These men make me happy. How can I trust you not to hurt me again if you won't let me be happy?"

At last, Axel nods, his troubled gaze searching mine. "I'm happy to have you in the pack, where I can keep you safe. You know that, Luna. And I do want you to be happy."

I raise my brows. "And my own house?"

"There's one down the block from me," he says, glowering like it offends him to think I'll have something of my own, separate from him. "Adolpha and her family need a bigger house."

"I remember her," I say, brightening. "She was nice."

"I'm sure she'd love to have you take over the place. She fixed it up real nice." Axel's face is hard, like stone.

"I can't wait to see it," I say, clapping my hands together. "My very own house, that I didn't have to build myself. I hope it has a tin roof like the one me and Mama had. I like the sound of the rain at night."

Axel's bruised jaw clenches. "When someone challenges the Alpha and loses, he's forced to leave the pack."

"And he did," I say. "But now he's coming back. I don't care if it's the werewolf law. We're outlaws. Ethan says that means we can do stuff other people think is bad, and we don't care."

"This will make you accept me as your mate again?" Axel asks, his miserable gaze on mine.

"It's a start," I say. "You can keep proving yourself, and one day, when I'm done forgiving you for hurting me and my wolf so bad, we can talk about whether you can be my mate again."

Axel looks like he might explode. Instead, like the Alpha he is, he stands up, and even though he's beaten and battered and has to limp across the room, he somehow still looks imposing as he stops in front of the triplets. The glare he gives them makes my wolf cower down inside me, begging for mercy even though he's not angry at us. "You are granted hunting rights to our share of Creebay Preserve," he says. "Don't fuck it up, and if you hurt Luna, I will disembowel all three of you and hang you by a noose made of your own intestines."

With that, he wheels around toward the door. My wolf cries for him to come back, and his wolf must feel it, because he glances over his shoulder with one long, searching gaze. My wolf blazes to life, eager to answer his every command. But he turns without a word and walks out the door.

# **Chapter Fourteen**

*Callan*

For the next week, we work on getting Luna settled into her new place and enjoy our newfound freedom to Jacksonville pack territory. Warrick's a dick about it, of course. He flaunts our ability to hunt on Creebay Preserve by going as near to the pack houses as possible to make a kill, marking his territory on every tree he trots past in wolf form, and roaring down Golden Glade Street on his motorcycle at all hours of the day or night when he's in human form.

When someone questions him the first time, he flashes his gap-toothed grin and says, "Why don't you and your Alpha have a little talk? He'll tell you we're welcome."

After that, no one bothers us. They don't talk to us, either.

165

Ethan's just as bad. Like now, when Axel stops by for the tenth time today, this time asking Luna if she needs her plumbing fixed or the boards on her deck looked over for signs of decay.

"We're taking care of her plumbing just fine," Ethan says, throwing his arm around Luna, who's standing near the counter, stacking her new dishes in the cupboard. "In fact, we take turns flushing the pipes four, five times a day. Don't we, darlin'?"

"I don't know," Luna says, a picture of wide-eyed innocence. "I haven't checked the pipes at all."

Ethan guffaws, and Axel glares.

Luna looks like an advertisement for domestic bliss standing in her kitchen, organizing all the items Axel bought for her. The kitchen has sunshiny yellow walls and curtains with sunflowers on them. New tile covers the floor, and her cupboards have been painted blue. It looks like something out of a damn magazine, and Luna loves it.

"Need anything?" Axel asks our pet, ignoring Ethan's crude comments. "I can stop by the grocery store if you do. Food, cleaning products, anything."

Luna taps her lips with her finger. "I do need a few things if you don't mind."

Axel brightens like she's granted him his wildest dream. In a way she has, since she's agreed to join his pack. If he was the one pounding her pussy every night, he'd be a happy man. But that joy belongs to our Alpha—Warrick. I'm amazed Axel has been so good-natured about the whole affair. He hasn't tried to take off any of our heads since our big fight a week ago. He probably doesn't know Warrick's nailing his mate every which way after Axel goes home to jerk off alone each evening.

After she tells Axel what groceries she needs, he heads off, and Ethan roars off on his bike to pick up a paycheck from our last job. I cross the blue and tan tile floor, reach into the box with the remaining plates and bowls, and start handing them to Luna.

She holds up one of the brown-rimmed, blue ceramic bowls. "Aren't these pretty? I picked them myself. Axel said I could have anything I wanted. Imagine!"

I glance at the bowl. What do I know about dishes? All I care about is that Luna likes them. "They're real nice," I say.

"You don't like them?" she says, sensing my indifference. Her full lips form a pout. "When I lived in the swamp with Mama, I never dreamed of owning something this pretty. We barely ever used a dish at all."

"I said they're pretty," I say, holding up a hand. "If you like 'em, I like 'em."

"What do you really think, though?" she asks, setting the bowl in the stack with the others. "I want your honest take."

"Luna," I say with a grin. "Plates are hardly on my radar. I don't give two shits whether they're made of pure gold or you don't use one at all. You, however, are a different story." I snake an arm around her waist and pull her into me. "I give lots of shits about you, pet."

The cutest blush colors her face. I kiss her warm cheek until she pushes me away. "Quit," she squeals. "I vowed to get all these dishes and pans put away before evening, which, in case you haven't noticed, is coming right up."

"That's why I'm helping you," I say, setting the stack of plates into the cabinet. "You need a break. Let me take you out tonight, Luna. A real date. My brothers can make their own dinner."

"What's a date?" she asks, her forehead furrowing.

"Something I haven't done in a long-ass time," I say with a grin, hefting a box of glassware onto the tan-tile countertop. "But it's when people are getting to know each other, and they go out and do fun things."

I slice open the box with a box cutter Axel got Luna. Dude thought of everything.

"Like when I went hunting with Axel," she says, her lilac eyes lighting up the way they do when she catches on. She fishes a blue glass from the box and sets it on a shelf in another cupboard.

"Sure." I hand her another glass. "Only on this date, we'll go into town. Maybe catch an old movie at the restored theater."

"What's a movie?" she asks, placing the glass next to the other one.

"It's like TV but bigger. We sit with a bunch of other people and watch the show together." I hand her the rest of the glasses and flatten the empty box, tossing it onto the pile of others.

"Oh," she says. "So more like when I met the pack, and we all ate dinner together instead of at home with just us." She arranges the glassware on the shelf in a neat row.

"That's a good way to put it," I say, smiling at her. "So, what do you say?"

"Okay," she says, standing on tiptoes to put up the last of the glasses. As her little body stretches, my cock throbs in my jeans. I've kept my hands off her since the day she woke up. I still need to tell Warrick about that. Luna rambles on, not noticing that I've fallen silent as I try to control the stiffy that's popped up from simply watching her do a mundane task. I want to fuck her again so bad it's a constant battle with blue balls.

"TV is funny," she says. "It don't make no sense to me. I don't even know those people. Why do I care about their stories? And then when I found out that half of them aren't even telling the truth?" She shakes her head, then turns to lean against the counter.

I shrug, resisting the urge to adjust myself. "It's entertainment."

"Then let's do it," Luna says with a bright smile, right as Axel strides through the door holding two bags overflowing with groceries.

"Where are y'all headed?" he asks, eyeing us with a frown. I can see it's eating the guy up that he can't be with Luna the way he wants. I almost feel for the asshole. Thanks to his wolf, the cuts and scrapes on his face are almost all healed, and he's back to looking like the perfect All-American asshole he is.

"To this thing called the movies," Luna says before I can stop her.

"You can't go to the movies," Axel says, setting the heavy bags on the kitchen table pushed against the wall.

"Why not?" she demands, crossing her arms over her chest.

*Oh, boy. Here we go.*

Axel and Luna have a tempestuous relationship if this week is any indication. They bicker all the time. I can't tell if it's foreplay building up to some big, explosive fuck-fest when they give in, or if they really can't stand each other despite wanting to fuck each other's brains out.

"It's not safe," Axel says flatly. "I only granted these assholes access to our territory because you agreed to move onto pack land where it's safe, and you'd be protected from lone wolves. The rest of Jacksonville isn't safe."

"How safe was I roaming the land when the lone wolf attacked me?"

"You weren't, which proves my point," Axel says, drawing himself up to his full height. "You weren't on pack land."

"I smelled the same wolf when we were out hunting at the preserve," she counters.

"What you smelled," Axel says, removing soup cans from the paper bag and slamming them on the counter.

"Was Warrick. He even told you he was out stalking you, spying on us. Probably jerking off like a fucking pervert."

"I know what Warrick smells like. It wasn't Warrick," Luna spits back at him.

"How do I know this asshole won't run off with you and take you somewhere to have you all to himself?" Axel growls.

"This asshole," I say, "has no intention of taking her away to have her all to himself. It's more fun to have her right under your nose, Alpha."

Axel rakes his hand through his hay-colored hair. I like rattling his cage—we all do. But he seems to be mastering the ability to not let us get to him, though I know the only reason he's holding back from ripping out my entrails is because he'd lose Luna forever if he killed one of us.

"You do seem to take pleasure in fucking with me," he says, glowering at me. "But it's still not a good idea to leave pack land. Even if that was a lone wolf and Warrick got rid of it, there are vampires, goblins, all kinds of shit that might hurt her out there."

"If you were so worried about it, maybe you shouldn't have invited them onto your territory," I point out. "By the way, they're not keeping to the north. I've seen at least one near here."

"Why didn't you tell me sooner?" Axel barks.

I shrug. "You're not my Alpha."

"This is my territory," he growls, squeezing the back of his neck.

"Axel," Luna says, laying a hand on his forearm. He drops his gaze to her fingers and swallows.

"No one else stays on pack land all the time. I want to go out with Callan, so I'm going. You can't protect me every second."

"Bullshit," he snarls.

Luna sighs and takes her touch from his arm. "Besides, I have Callan with me. He'll protect me. If my safety is what you're really worried about, then you can't object."

"The girl's decided, *Dad,*" I say sarcastically. "I'll make sure she's home by midnight."

"You better be damn sure she's safe," he growls. "Protect her with your fucking life, because I'll end it if something happens to her."

I grin and shake my head, laying an arm over Luna's shoulders and puffing up my chest. "I don't need you to tell me to keep her safe. Again, you ain't my Alpha, so you don't run the show where we're concerned."

"Boys, boys," Luna says, stepping between us. "Don't fight. Please?"

She looks up at me with her little puppy dog eyes that make my dick hard and my defenses crumble. Then she turns to give Axel the same look. He sighs. It's the weapon of a submissive wolf—they're anything but weak. She may be naïve, but she's not dumb. She's learning fast, and I have no doubt that within a year, she'll have us all eating out of her hand and doing anything we can to earn one of her smiles or a night between her heavenly thighs.

"Good," she says, laying a hand on Axel's chest. "Then it's settled. Callan will protect me if anything goes wrong."

"Fine," Axel says grudgingly, sending me a fierce scowl. "I've got to consult with my wolves about the vampires encroaching. They're already pissed about having them on half the preserve, and if they're not respecting our boundaries…"

I can feel his wolf surging, the instinctual urge to fight rising inside him. My own wolf responds even though I'm not under his command and not bonded to the pack, so I can't read his thoughts. I can still feel a stronger wolf's agitation. I have to remind my wolf to stand down, that this isn't our battle, and we don't care about his pack's land.

Distracted by his concerns for the pack, Axel leaves Luna to me. Forty-five minutes later, we're standing in line at the movie theater, waiting to buy tickets. Luna and I are holding hands like a couple of teenagers. Well, I guess Luna is a teenager, as uncomfortable as that makes me. But it's too late to back out now. She's got me—hook, line, and sinker.

"I haven't been to the movies since I was in high school," I say, wrapping an arm around her shoulders.

"What's high school?" she says, snuggling into the crook of my arm.

"It's where you go learn bullshit you'll never use," I say with a grin. "I barely went."

"Why would you want to learn something you don't need to?"

"My thoughts exactly."

Luna gawks at all the people around us and presses into me, clearly uncomfortable with this crowd. "Were the movies part of it?" she asks. "Because if they're like TV, I don't see the use."

"You could say that," I admit with a grin. "Getting my cock sucked in the back row was definitely more memorable than most of the shit that happened during those years."

"You can suck a cock?" Luna asks, all wide-eyed innocence.

"You sure can, pet," I say. "I'll let you suck mine as soon as the movie starts."

"Can we fuck again, too?"

"If you can stay quiet, you might be able to slide that pussy down over my dick," I say with a wink. "If not, you'll have to settle for making out."

"What's making out?"

"This is making out." I tip up her chin with my fingertip and lower my lips to hers.

Our lips grind together until the prick behind us says, "Hey, buddy, move."

"Yeah, fuck you," I say, not bothering to look at him. Instead, I slide a hand down the back of Luna's pants, cupping her tight little ass as we take a few steps forward.

"I like making out, too," she says, her eyes all bright with excitement. "But not as much as fucking."

"Keep that talk up and we won't make it through the credits before I'm wrecking your ass."

"This date is sounding more and more fun," Luna says.

"I couldn't agree more," I murmur against her ear. "I've been dreaming of being inside that tight pussy again all week."

I step up to the ticket booth, hand the cashier a card, and pay for our tickets, keeping my hard-on pushed up tight against Luna's back.

"What are we going to watch when we're not fucking?" Luna asks.

I almost bust up laughing when the pimply little pipsqueak behind the register turns ten shades of red. Apparently we forgot to teach Luna about appropriate voice levels when talking about pussy in public.

When we walk away from the ticket counter, I crack up and laugh my ass off. I can't remember the last time I had this much fun. Maybe never. Sure, I like to come as much as the next guy, but I'm usually on the serious side. Luna brings out something else in me, though, letting me feel carefree and young, pussy-whipped and about head over fucking paws for the rest of her, too.

# **Chapter Fifteen**

*Luna*

Living in a real house with rugs instead of rags on a floor made of wood instead of dirt, with walls instead of tin and plastic we found in the swamp... It takes a bit of getting used to, but luckily, I've been eased in by living with the triplets and Axel. But this house isn't one that belongs to someone else, where I'm a guest. It's *mine*.

I can't believe I can call something so lovely my own.

Best of all, I get to say who comes and goes instead of Axel or Warrick making the rules. In this one little place in the world, no matter how submissive my wolf is, I am an Alpha. This is my domain, and I treasure its beauty like the miraculous gift that it is.

The triplets still have their home in the deep woods, of course. Warrick says a man needs his space. But they spend so much time in my house that I forget we don't all live here. Axel stops by each day, too. He brings me anything I need, fixes every loose floorboard and shutter, and does whatever I ask. Maybe he thinks I'm an Alpha, too.

I'm both pleased and hurt by the fact that he never tries to touch me again. His actions convey the world about his character and how much I mean to him, though, even if I don't know what made him stop wanting to fuck me. I still want to fuck him—a lot. That time in the woods, when his knot filled me up until I thought I'd tear in two, was the most intense physical sensation I've ever had.

Even though Warrick is big, and he satisfies me completely, I'm curious to try the knot thing again. Warrick says he can't do that, though. Only a True Mate can. And Axel seems uninterested in trying again. In fact, when I hint at it one evening, he leaves like I spooked him as much as the wolf watching us in the woods spooked me.

Still, I know he must care about me in other ways, since he gave me my beautiful home. I keep it in tip-top shape and sparkling clean, which is hard with the three oafs who have taken it over with their muddy boots and stray socks and beer cans. One afternoon I'm doing something called vacuuming with a device that sucks up dirt, running it over the rug in my living, when a paper cup of coffee appears in front of my face.

"Oh!" I cry, dropping the vacuum and jumping back.

Axel bends to pick up the vacuum and turns it off, setting it upright. "I knocked," he says with a small smile. "I heard the vacuum and figured you didn't hear me. Seemed safe enough to let myself in. None of those heathens would be cleaning, so I figured I wouldn't find you..." His smile falters, and he doesn't finish his sentence.

I wonder what he was afraid he'd find me doing.

He whips a colorful bouquet of wildflowers from behind his back. "I thought you might like these, too. They're just for decoration, not to eat. Brighten up the place, that kind of thing."

"Oh, thank you!" I cry. "They're perfect."

Axel smiles at my appreciation, watching me take a sniff of each different one.

I pull a ceramic vase from the cupboard over the sink and fill it with water before plunking in the orange, yellow and white blossoms. Then I just stand there, not sure what to do with it. Axel takes it gently and sets it on the kitchen table, which I see immediately is the right place. They look right at home and make the room even prettier.

Axel looks at me, standing uneasily in the center of the room. Then I remember what he told me about manners—that it's polite to ask if people want something when they come over. Civilized people expect more than sniffs and licks when they stop over. They want something called hospitality. The triplets didn't teach me that, since Axel says they don't know the meaning of the term. Even though he doesn't like the triplets, I take his word for it, because they mostly killed anyone who came by their house when I lived there.

Apparently other people offer tea.

"Can I get you something to drink?" I ask, the way he taught me.

He arches a brow and holds up his coffee cup, a cardboard one that matches the one he gave me. "I can't stay long," he says. "I've got pack business to attend to. Just wanted to bring you something pretty to look at."

"Thanks," I say, hopping up on a bar stool and picking up my coffee. "How's it going with the pack?"

Axel sighs and leans against the wall, wrapping one arm across his flat stomach to hold the opposite elbow. "Not too good," he admits, taking a swig of coffee. "Everyone's uneasy with vampires roaming Creebay and your guys moving in here. They could understand you coming back, but the triplets were part of the pack once, and they chose to leave."

"It's my house," I say. "I don't know why anyone cares if they're in my house."

"Because they know you're my mate, Luna," Axel says. "It looks all kinds of fucked up for my mate to be entertaining my enemies right under my nose, and them flaunting it in my face, and me not doing a goddamn thing about it."

"You agreed they could come on pack land."

"And I stand by that," he says, holding up his free hand. "I've explained it to the pack as my gesture of goodwill after what I did, but some of them don't think I'm fit to lead if I'll let that go on and not put a stop to it. And when an Alpha's warriors start to think he looks weak, it's the end of him. Anarchy creeps in, and the next thing you know, some asshole like Warrick is challenging me for Alpha again."

"Am I really worth all this trouble you've gotten yourself into?" I say, curling my legs under the chair and hooking my toes around the crossbar on the chair.

"Yes."

My heart expands to fill the room.

Before I can tell Axel how happy that makes me, back door opens and thwacks shut, and Ethan strolls into the kitchen, shirtless and glistening with sweat. He looks so good my tongue wants to loll out like my wolf is eyeing a fresh kill.

He catches my lusty gaze and grins. "Garden's all dug up and ready for planting."

"Thank you," I say, watching him wipe his forehead with one of my kitchen towels.

He tosses it on the counter and leans against the stove, his tattooed, bulging muscles on full display. When his attention swings toward Axel, his grin turns wicked. "And here's the mutt who keeps sniffing around like you're a bitch in heat."

"Hello to you, too, Ethan," Axel says wryly, not rising to the bait. He turns toward me. "That's where we're at with the pack. Constantly putting out fires. I'll see you later, Luna."

He gives me a kiss on the forehead and Ethan a nod he doesn't deserve before ducking out the front door and pulling it shut behind him.

I wish the triplets would be nicer to Axel, but I'm not sure what I can do about it. I already told them, and they didn't listen. Ethan saunters toward me, scoops me up off the barstool, tosses me over his shoulder, and heads for the living room. He flops onto the couch with me and pulls me into his lap. The scent of musk pouring off him makes me instantly aroused.

He nibbles at my neck, his scratchy beard tickling my skin. "So, beautiful… When do you go into heat? Because you're going to have to tell me and Callan ahead of time so we can hole up at our old place beforehand unless you want me to fill you with a whole litter of puppies."

"What?" I ask, twisting around on his lap.

"Come on, Luna. Now that you're a good little housewife, Warrick's going to want to breed you right to prove you're his. The pack's really going to lose their shit over that."

He chuckles and grips my hips, moving me around on his cock.

"What do you mean?" I wrap my arms around his neck and blink up at him. "I'm not Warrick's. I'm all of yours."

"Does Warrick know that?" Ethan asks, running his hand up and down my shorts-clad thigh.

"Well… I mean… I think so?"

"Don't get me wrong, I like our little stolen moments like this, but he'd rip my throat out if he saw you grinding on my dick like this. Totally worth the blueballs for me, but you might want to tell him if you're not serious about him. He definitely thinks it's more than just fucking."

"It is," I say, thinking of how nice it feels to curl my little body up against his huge one every night, to feel protected and treasured as he holds me in the crook of his arm after fucking me hard and calling me his baby girl while he comes so deep inside me that I can't even breathe.

"You don't understand relationships at all, do you?" Ethan asks, grinning at me while he pushes his hips up under me.

"No," I admit. "Not really."

"Well, let's just say that you'd better tell him you're not his alone before you go into heat if you don't want a bloodbath on your hands. Every unmated male wolf will be howling at your door, and I'm sure as fuck going to put my seed in you if you let me."

"Warrick did say I should wear clothes when I'm home so y'all and the rest of the pack aren't panting after me, but I didn't really know what he meant," I say. The heat level has been unbearable, and it's all I can do to wear any clothes at all. Warrick used his wolf dominance to stress the importance, though, and all of Axel's pack wears clothes. I've been doing my best to keep them on, so I fit in when I'm ready to go out into the pack again.

"Haven't you ever been in heat before?" Ethan asks,

"Once," I say, stroking the fur on his leg. "Mama got a witch to make them stop, but Axel gave me something to take the spell off when I was staying there. I don't think it worked, though, because I haven't gone into heat yet."

"I'm glad we didn't miss it." Ethan eyes my lips with intense, feral hunger. "What happened when you were in heat before?"

"Mama tried to keep me locked up our little house, but it wasn't built to withstand anything, and I kept escaping. I didn't know what I needed, exactly, just that I had this heat between my legs that ached so bad, and that I had to find a way to put out the fire."

"Did you touch yourself?" Ethan asks, his eyes blazing with desire.

"Some, but it didn't help much," I say. "And then it started to hurt because I did it too much. Mama took me to the hot springs and told me to soak it off, but it only helped as long as I was in the water. The second I got out, the need would be back."

"Oh, baby, I can't wait for that to happen." Ethan guides my body until I'm straddling him, pushed against his rigid length. "Feel that, sweetheart. I'm going to help you quench that fire all day when you're in heat. I just hope I'm the one who gets a baby in you."

He palms my belly before pulling my head in to meet his lips.

We make out—my new favorite term after the movies with Callan—for a few minutes. Our tongues collide and caress as Ethan thrusts his cock against my core. At last, he slides my shorts aside and sinks a finger into my wet pussy. His eyes roll back, and he groans.

"Want to start practicing now, so we're ready when it comes?"

I laugh. "We could. But first, I have a question."

"What is it?" he asks, pumping his finger into me slowly.

The sensation scrambles my brain. I arch into him, panting for more. "How can I think of what I want to ask when you're doing that?"

"That's my plan." He leans forward and bites my neck, adding a second finger to the first that's gliding in and out of me. "If you're not just Warrick's, this pussy's mine for the fucking."

Mercy on the swamp dogs, it feels go good I almost lose my mind.

"What's your question?" he whispers into my skin.

"Have you ever done that before?" I ask. "Got a baby in someone?"

"No," he murmurs against my neck. "I never wanted to before you."

"Why not?"

He shrugs. "Growing up with a son of a bitch for a father didn't leave me keen to sire my own offspring. I figured I'd only fuck them up. None of the women I've known were interested in anything but having their brains fucked out, and that's all I was after, so everybody wins."

"I see," I say, as a sudden jab of jealousy stabs at my insides.

"I don't think you do, pup," Ethan says, circling his fingers inside me until my eyes roll back and my hips buck involuntarily against him. "I've seen that expression on you before, and I can assure you there's nothing you need to worry about. I never cared for a woman before, but now that I've met you, I want things I never dreamed I'd want. I don't even remember a single one of those women's names. When I try, I just think of you."

I start to melt in his lap at his declaration and the magic spell his fingers are casting. I feel utterly delicious hearing that Ethan's never before felt what he feels for me.

"You gonna come on my fingers, or am I going to have to pound you with my cock to get you off?" he asks, his breath coming fast as he rocks his hips against my ass in rhythm with his pumping fingers.

"Your cock," I moan, reaching for the button of his jeans.

Just as I'm about to slide my hand inside, a knock sounds at the door, interrupting us.

"Luna?" Axel says, easing open the door and sticking his head inside. "Are you still here? I wanted to talk to you."

# **Chapter Sixteen**

*Luna*

Axel steps inside as I scramble from Ethan's lap. I button my shorts, pat my hair, and smooth the front of my lavender top, trying to bring order to my appearance before turning to face my Alpha.

"Axel," I say. "What are you doing here?" I stand beneath the overhead fan, enjoying how it cools my flushed skin. The temperature outside must be approaching one-hundred, and it's muggy from the swamp, making us all damp and sticky.

"What do you mean?" Axel's gaze slides back and forth between Ethan and me. He looks hot and grumpy as he stands in my tiny foyer, as if it offends him that I'm with someone besides Warrick. Which doesn't make sense, because he hates Warrick most of all.

I'm afraid I will never understand this thing called relationships.

"I come by every day," Axel says. "Am I interrupting?"

"No," I say, just as Ethan says, "Yes."

Ethan's fly is hanging open, and I want to stand in front of him, so Axel doesn't notice. I'm not sure why, because I know Axel won't tell Warrick before I get the chance. Ethan makes no attempt to zip up, and his cock bulges against his jeans. He lounges on the couch, his arm resting along the back.

Axel's mouth works back and forth as he regards the two of us. "What's going on, Luna?" he asks, looking... Hurt, I think.

I'm still learning to read his expressions, but I can tell he's trying to hide it. His wolf isn't doing as well at appearing unbothered, though.

Ethan palms his erection. "What's it look like? Do you think I get this hard over the furniture?"

I could just about slug him. He's constantly tormenting Axel.

"Ethan, don't," I say. "There's no need to stir up trouble."

He grins up at Axel, ignoring me. "Yeah, okay, little pup. Let's not stir up trouble for the guy who's constantly checking up on you. She's fine, asshole, and she'd be even finer if you hadn't just stopped her from getting wrecked by the best dick of her life."

Axel gives me a wounded look. "I thought…"

"What?" Ethan asks, giving Axel a savage grin. "That because she's your mate, we wouldn't pass her around every night so we can all get a turn to come in that tight little pussy? Come on, now. You know our reputation. Surely that's all we know how to do with a woman."

Axel swallows, the little Adam's apple lump on his throat moving up and down, his eyes fixed on Ethan. I can feel pain radiating off him, and I don't like it.

"Ethan, stop," I say. "Axel, that's not true. Only Warrick comes in my pussy every night."

I'm not sure what I said wrong, but Axel looks like he's in danger of wolfing out and tearing Ethan's head off.

"Maybe you should go out back for a minute," I say to Ethan.

"Fuck this guy. I'm going for a ride," Ethan says. "Want to join me?"

"I need to talk to you, Luna," Axel says. "Before you head out with… Whatever this guy is to you."

"Let me see what he wants, and then we can go for a ride," I say to Ethan, desperately trying to make him happy and not make Axel sad at the same time.

"Nah. You do your thing with this asshole, and I'll catch up with you later," Ethan says. He grabs his black leather biker's vest off the living room chair where he deposited it earlier. Before heading out, he leans down to give me a soft kiss on the lips and chucks me on the chin. Then he skewers Axel with his hateful gaze before striding out the front door.

An awkward tension stretches between Axel and me.

"Can I get you anything? Beer? Water?" I ask, practicing the new social manners he taught me. Maybe if I show him that I'm using what he gave me, he'll feel better.

"Let's go for a walk," he says, taking a few sniffs of the air. "I need to get outside."

"Sure," I say, since by afternoon, it's hotter inside my house than out. I can smell what he does, the scent of my arousal perfuming the air around us.

"You have everything you need here?" Axel asks as we step onto the porch. The sky is darkening in the east, but the air is still, with a restless, irritable charge. Definitely a storm coming.

"Yes, Axel," I say. "You've been getting my every need met before I even know I have it—buying me dishes, towels, groceries… I do appreciate it."

"All of your needs," he says, his mouth in a sour twist. "You mean your material needs, right?"

"Exactly," I say as we start along Golden Glade Street. The sidewalk shimmers from the heat, and I hope my sandals don't melt. Wearing shoes has taken some getting used to, but sidewalks retain heat like crazy. No way could I place my feet or my wolf paws on this searing concrete. The palm trees lining the road do nothing to shield us from the thick, sweltering air.

The further we get away from my house, the more Axel seems to settle. He leads me along a path into the woods, so we're not baking in the sun. "So," he says. "You like the new place?"

"Oh, I love it!" I say, my mood lifting instantly. "I never owned anything so amazing in my life."

This statement seems to please him, as evidenced by the smile on his face. But after a few minutes of padding along the dirt path in silence, his frown returns. "Are you fucking them?" he asks. "I want to hear it from you."

"Do you *really* want to know?" I ask, my mood turning south, too.

"No," he admits, his jaw set as he stares blankly into the distance.

"How'd it go with the pack?" I ask, hoping to circumvent what will surely turn into a fight if we continue down the track of what I'm up to with the three brothers.

"As well as could be expected, what with you living here, the triplets living here, and the vamps occupying so much territory... Ethan was right about the vampires not sticking to the territory I gave them."

"I know he likes to lie to make you mad," I say. "But I didn't think that was a lie."

Axel rubs the back of his neck before continuing. "Woulda been helpful if he'd told me sooner. But I know things are strained between us."

"I'm sorry about that," I say. "I can't seem to stop making chaos wherever I go."

"It's not your fault, Luna," he says, casting a long, wistful glance in my direction. "How could it not be tense? We all want the same thing—you."

"I know," I say. "It's so hard to figure out what to do. I want... I just want everyone to be happy. And once I learned what jealousy was, it don't seem like that's possible. If more than one person wants the same thing, it sure gets complicated."

"It could be simple," he says, snagging my hand. He waits, as if he thinks I'll pull away, but my wolf is thrilling inside me at his touch.

Axel stops and pulls me in closer, turning to face me. "I'm still your mate, Luna," he says. "No matter how much you deny it. I know your wolf feels it, too. No one would argue that—even Warrick let us be together when he thought it's what you wanted…"

"But it's not what I want," I say, pulling myself away from him. "I want the triplets."

"Do you?" he asks, cocking his head. "Or are you just punishing me for severing our bond?"

I turn and stomp deeper into the woods, smelling fresh water ahead.

"Luna," Axel calls, hurrying after me. When I don't answer, he falls into step beside me. "You heading for the pond?"

"Is that what you wanted to talk to me about?" I demand, stomping across the pine needles and dead palm leaves to reach a murky, shallow pond.

I kick off my shoes and wade into the knee-deep water. It's brackish and slightly warm, but at least it's wet. And wading through the water helps me feel my natural self, the one I was in the swamp with Mama. Once I reach the middle of the pond, I sit down in the silty mud.

Axel laughs and shakes his head. "You're a trip, Luna. You're the only person I know who would sit in the middle of this pond with your clothes still on."

"Fuck clothes," I say. "I wish I could strip mine off, but you and the others made it clear I'm to act civilized here in town." I splash him with a scoop of water when he wades close enough for me to reach. "Are you going to loom over me, or are you going to join me?"

After a second, he grins and plunks down beside me, splashing me back.

We laugh and splash for a few minutes until we're both completely doused with water. Then, I lay back in the shallow pond and let myself float, my hair spreading around me like blue clouds across the sky.

Axel watches with soft eyes.

"What?" I ask, spreading my arms in the water like a water bug.

"I'd like to offer you a position in the pack, Luna," he says. "Will you be my Second?"

# **Chapter Seventeen**

*Luna*

"You want me to be your Second-in-Command?" I ask, gaping at Axel. "What about Ama?"

We're still sitting in the pond off of Golden Glades Street, surrounded by marsh plants and a few palm trees. Paper cups and food wrappers float along the edges, having blown in from town, but I don't have to scavenge for plastic cups or water jugs anymore, so I don't pay the trash any mind. While Axel speaks, I let my hands swirl lazily in the pea-green water.

"Ama and I are two very dominant wolves," Axel says. "It wouldn't hurt to have a more submissive wolf to tame the tempers of the rest of us."

I smile at Axel. I'm flattered to be offered a job in the pack and even more happy that he's getting rid of Ama. I don't like her one bit.

"What would I have to do?"

"You'll be my right-hand wolf," he says. "You'll help me make decisions on what's best for the pack, and you can even govern in my absence for a short time."

"Really?" I say, my eyes widening. "So, I can boss around the entire pack when you're not there? Is that what Ama does?"

Axel gives me an indulgent smile. "It's not exactly 'bossing around.' They look to you for guidance, order, structure, and protection. And, yes, that's Ama's role in the pack." The corners of his lips turn down. "But I think she might be good in a different role."

"What kind of role is that?" I ask, trying on the role of Second in my mind. I like the idea of having authority in the pack, but then again, it also sounds like responsibility that I'm not sure I'm ready for. I don't know any of the rules and laws like Ama does.

"To be Second, you'll need to accept the pack bond and become an official member." Axel's face almost glows with excitement. "You'll be bonded to all of the Jacksonville pack, even communicate with us telepathically if you're in any trouble. The Alpha and his Second have an even stronger bond. We'll be able to communicate just between the two of us, too."

"Wait a minute..." My eyes narrow. "Was this all a ploy to get me to join the pack so you can basically be my mate without being my mate?"

"It's not like that," he growls. "I want to keep you safe."

"Isn't it like that, though?" I ask, my relaxation from a moment ago melting as my spine stiffens into a steel rod. "It sure sounds like it. 'Hey, Luna, you can be my Second-in-Command and have an important role, but with one little catch. You're going to have to become a member of the pack and share a special bond with me.' That sounds just like being your *mate*." The word leaves a bitter taste in my mouth after all I've been through because of it.

"You can't be the pack's Second if you're not in the pack," he says, looking at me like I'm looney. "The Alpha and his Second have to be able to communicate during times of crisis to help the pack."

"And here I thought your offer was a gesture of goodwill."

"Who says it isn't?" he says, his golden eyes flashing fire.

"Your offer *stinks*. Being your Seconds sounds just like being your mate."

I frown, thinking of Ama carrying that much responsibility and having such a close bond with Axel. I don't like thinking about how close they are, how much they share that I'm not a part of because I don't belong to the pack yet. That's my choice, but I still don't like her around him.

"Fuck, Luna," Axel says with a sigh of frustration. "Of course I want you in the pack. I want you to be my mate. You *know* this. I never hid it. You're my fucking heartbeat itself. Every breath I take is an homage to you. I can't exist if you're not in my life, in whatever capacity I can have you, even if you're with those assholes instead of me. But I'm not going to trick you into being my mate."

Our eyes lock in a tangle of still-fresh wounds at this declaration. I don't know what to say. I might have grown to feel that way had the True Mate bond not been severed, but it was. Can I still feel like that now, after he hurt me so much? I don't like the thought of him with Ama, but that doesn't mean I want him for myself. Does it?

Doesn't Axel occupy a portion of my daily musings, whether I like it or not? He comes by every day, brings me things, dotes on me. I appreciate all the little gestures, the things he does to show he's sorry and let me know he's thinking about me all through the day. I feel *something* for him, I'm just not sure what it is.

"Look," he says, lifting his hands from the pond. Water drips down his arms. "Despite my personal desires, that choice is up to you. I won't force you to be my mate. That's separate from this. But either way, even if you're never mine again, you should join the pack."

"So you can read my mind?" I ask, thinking of how many times Mama told me not to trust wolves. If I can't keep a secret from them, I've trusted them completely.

Axel rakes a hand through his hair and blows out a breath. "You'll be safer in the pack. We protect each other. Imagine how being able to communicate with just a cry in your mind might have served you when that lone wolf attacked you. I'd have known the instant you were in danger, and believe me, I would have come running. All of the pack would have. We'd know your whereabouts, what you were experiencing, *everything.*"

I chew on my lip, considering. "I don't know nothing about the law," I say. "Pack law."

He sits forward. "I'll teach you. Pack history, pack law, hierarchy, all you need to know to help me lead and be my Second. What do you say, Luna?"

I ripple my fingers in the water as I consider the request while Axel waits. "Too much responsibility," I say at last. "Even I know you're not doing this for the pack. Even if you're not doing it to trick me, you're trying to give me the best things so I'll forgive you for doing the worst things. The answer's still no."

His entire body sags, like sand's draining from his bones.

"But I'll join the pack," I pronounce.

"Really?" he asks, his eyes brightening and a smile starting at the corners of his mouth.

"If my mates can join, too."

"What?" he demands. "What the fuck, Luna? Warrick challenged me for Alpha and lost. He was banished. The other two chose to sever their pack bonds. They can't just stroll back in like nothing happened."

"Why not?"

"If I let them come back after that, I'd look weak. In a lot of packs, a fight for Alpha is a fight to the death. Warrick's lucky he only got banished. If I let him come back, no one will ever take me seriously again."

"Why is it always about what the pack thinks of you?" I ask. "I thought you were their leader. Why does it matter what they think? You make the rules."

"I make rules for the good of my pack."

"And I make rules for the good of mine," I say, climbing to my feet. Pond water trickles down my legs and plops in drips from the hems of my shorts and shirt, making them heavy and tight. I want to peel them off, but

Warrick forbid me from going outside without clothes. I pivot and start back toward my house.

When I glance over my shoulder, Axel's not following me. He stands still, as if his feet are glued to the mud in the middle of the pond. I'm almost out of view when he shouts for me to wait.

I whip around and stare at him as he rushes toward me, water dripping off his clothes, too. "What am I waiting for?" I ask.

"I'll give you what you want," he says, holding out a hand as if to stop me from walking away again. "I'll do it. They can join the pack, too, if you'll join it. That's how much I want to keep you safe, Luna. I'd give anything to protect you. Even my reputation."

"I still don't want to be your Second," I warn. "But if my mates can join, too, then we'll all be safe."

"They're not your mates," he grits out.

"They're my mates if I say they are," I say, crossing my arms over my chest.

Axel's wolf howls inside him, but I can hear it. His furious protests tear at my heart with knives of guilt and longing. He wants me to be *his* mate—and my wolf wants that, too.

"So, I give you everything, and I get nothing," Axel says dully. "That's where we are now."

"You can stay for dinner," I offer.

"Dinner," Axel says flatly. "That's what you're willing to give?"

# Chapter Eighteen

*Warrick*

I got six dead swamp rabbits draped over the back of my bike, and I'm eager to share them with the family—until I spot that dickwad Axel, strolling next to Luna like they're a couple teenagers courting. I fix a steely-eyed glare at him until he and Luna are within a few feet of me.

"You just can't stay away, can you, puppy-dog?" I growl at him. "Sniffing around here like she's a bitch in heat. Pathetic."

I'd rip his throat out if I could walk out of here alive, but I know the pack would kill me and my brothers too if I touched their fucking Alpha. I'm so sick of his ugly mug showing up day and night, mooning over my Luna, it'd almost be worth it.

Luna sidles over to me and gives me a sweet kiss, trying to sooth my temper. I heft the rope-bound dead rabbits from my bike and hold them up like a prize. "See what I caught for you, baby girl?" I say, dismissing Axel from my line of sight. "Your man brought home food to feed the family."

"Thank you," she says, her eyes lighting up.

I sling my other arm over her shoulder, effectively pushing Axel out of the way. I sneer at him before speaking. "Food I hunted, not just bought from the grocery store."

"That's great, Warrick," Luna chirps. "Axel's joining us, and it looks like you brought home enough for all of us."

Her statement grinds in my gears. I didn't spend the whole day in the preserve chasing these dumb bunnies through the marsh only to share my hard work with the likes of Axel. "What a good idea, Luna," I say, my teeth bared in a snarl at Axel. "Maybe he'll get it through his head that your ass is mine now, and he'll stop mooning over you like he's got a shot."

I kiss her thoroughly just to rub it in his face. He needs to know he's never getting her back. When I pull away, Luna giggles breathlessly. I smirk down at her. "You have a good day, baby girl?"

"I did have a good day," she says, smiling and snuggling into my side, where she's tucked into the protection of my arm.

"Same here." I lift the rabbits again and give the bundle of meat a wiggle. "These fuckers are wily."

"Don't I know it," she says. "I caught them for Mama and me when we lived alone. It was more fun catching Key deer with Axel, though." Her eyes sparkle at the memory, and my wolf growls inside me.

"They're hardly a sporting challenge," I say, shooting Axel a superior look. "All Key deer do is huddle together with the rest of the pack like sheep. These little guys give you a run for your money."

"They're hardly sheep," Axel mutters. "We felled a buck. Luna and I worked as a team to take him down."

I give Luna a little squeeze as we tromp up the porch stairs. Reaching for the door handle, I hold it open for her, then slide in front of Axel and release the door, so he has to catch it before it clocks him in the face.

"Callan!" I bellow when I've stepped onto Luna's tiny foyer.

"What's up?" he calls from the living room. "I'm kicking Ethan's ass in this game."

"Get your ass out here and make us some supper," I growl. "Luna's invited a *guest.*"

I tromp into the kitchen and spread the rabbits out on the counter. Then, I head to the fridge and retrieve a cold brew for myself and hold out one to Luna. "Want one?"

"I'm good," she says as she shuffles toward the counter to start the rabbit prep. "Axel?"

"Sure. I'll take one." Axel gives me a cool look, trying to fucking lord his dominance over me in my own mate's house.

"Nah," I say, closing the fridge and leaning on the counter. "That's a waste of good beer."

I tip back my head and take a few long swallows, watching the priceless look of utter, impotent fury on Axel's face from the corner of my eye. Then I step behind Luna and massage the back of her neck with my free hand.

"Mmm. That feels good," she says, laying the rabbits out.

"Good," I say, pushing aside her long hair to kiss her neck. "Call it pre-foreplay. It's to get you ready for foreplay, which is to get you ready for what I'm packing."

A pretty blush colors her cheeks while Axel's face grows apoplectic red.

It makes me want to laugh—it's so damn easy to get his goat. I head to the table, sit down, and lean back on the back two legs, enjoying myself immensely. If he's going to keep harassing my mate after we both told him to shove a dick up his ass, I'll remind him exactly how thoroughly he fucked up.

Luna opens a drawer and retrieves a shiny cleaver. Placing the first carcass on the cutting board, she chops off all four legs at the ankles, then slices off the tail and the head. Pulling the skin away from the belly, she takes a smaller knife and cuts apart the hide from groin to neck, careful to not pierce the stomach. Now she's ready to peel away the skin like she's removing a tight coat from the carcass.

I like watching her. Her focus and skill with a sharp blade make my wolf swell with pride.

*Mine.*

She carefully guts the rabbit, then removes its liver, which she places on a plate.

"You want the organ meat?" she asks me.

I shoot Axel a grin, and Luna's eyes fly wide. Maybe she thinks since he's the Alpha, he should get the organs. But Axel's status ain't shit in this house, and he knows it. He's leaning against the wall all casual-like, but what he sees in here must burn like a brand to his soul.

"Sure, baby girl," I say. "Bring it to me."

After presenting the liver to me, Luna affords Axel another glance, this one laced with what looks like sympathy. He doesn't react, but I know his wolf's seething inside. What Alpha male in his right mind wouldn't care when the woman he longs for serves up the best bits to another man? And I'm not just getting the best bits of the rabbit. I get the best bits of her.

"Thanks, darlin'," I say to her before picking up the raw liver with my fingers and popping it in my mouth. I chew slowly, watching the vein in Axel's head tick with each heartbeat.

As Luna finishes prepping the carcasses, Callan strides in with a grin on his face. "Now that I'm done kicking Ethan's ass," he says, talking about his dumbass video game. "Step aside for the master chef, pet."

Luna giggles and steps out of the way, taking the entrails to the trash.

"Callan," Axel says with a nod.

The poor guy's out of his league here. He must be dying a thousand deaths to witness the easy way all of us interact with Luna.

Callan prepares the rabbit stew and Luna cleans up, the two of them keeping up an easy banter all the while. Ethan joins and makes a salad while I have a cigarette at the table. None of us pay Axel any mind. Luna tries to include him in any conversations, but the rest of us cut him out. No one asked him to be here.

After we're all seated and the meal is served, we dig in. For a few minutes, none of us speak as we wolf down the food. Axel sets down his spoon halfway through his bowl, like he's been looking for his balls the whole time. He frowns at Luna and then turns to us.

"I'd like to extend an invitation," he says. "For you to join the pack."

No one says a word.

My brothers both turn their gazes to me, though. I slurp up a spoonful of soup.

"It's because I asked him to," Luna bursts out. "Axel can change pack law. He's the Alpha. And the pack *can* offer us protection."

"We didn't ask him to change anything," Ethan says. "We're fine with the way things stand."

Callan scratches his beard. "Can't say we need your protection," he says to Axel. "We've been getting along just fine without y'all for the past ten-plus years."

Axel blows out a lungful of air. "Yeah, I get that," he says, looking pissed. "You wouldn't benefit that much. But think of Luna—the pack can telepathically communicate with her if she's in trouble. Think of how that might have saved her from nearly dying a couple of weeks ago."

"I think we managed," I say, picking up my soup bowl and downing the rest of the contents in a few big swallows. I wipe my mouth on the back of my hand and glare at him.

"You can manage better with the pack, and we all know it," Axel states, placing his palms on the table. "I won't beg. But it's the only way Luna will join. I'm willing to share my pack, the protection it offers, and all that goes along with it for her sake."

"You just want to fuck her," Ethan says.

Axel's lips purse, but he keeps his cool.

"You already shared your mate with us," I say with a grin, enjoying goading the asshole. "It's a good thing, too, or she'd never know what it was like to be fucked by a real man."

I pull out my tobacco and start to roll up a cigarette.

"She's not your mate," Axel states, his fingers pressing into the table so that the muscles in his forearm bulge.

I light my cigarette and blow a cloud of smoke at him.

"She chose me as her mate," I say. "Now she's mine."

"Please don't fight," Luna says, her appeasing nature surfacing. "We all share everything. If I join the pack, I want to share that with y'all, too."

"We don't share *everything*," I growl. "Not with him."

"But we all share with each other," Luna says. "Me and you and your brothers. Our own little pack."

"That's right." I crush out my cigarette and grin at her, eyeing her tight little body. "I'm your Alpha and your mate. Your ass is mine now, not his. Which means I can share you however I see fit, with whomever I see fit."

Luna nods eagerly. "Yes, I'm yours," she agrees.

I pull her from her chair and onto my lap, hook my hand behind her neck, and lower my mouth to hers. I can't remember the last time I kissed a woman—it's been years. I fuck Luna near every night, but kissing isn't something that interests me. But tonight, I kiss her with fury and longing and lucifer be damned, how she responds. Her little hands grip my arms as I plunge my tongue rhythmically against hers, my cock stiffening under her ass until she's squirming and panting.

When I draw back, she's positively glowing, flushed with desire, and everyone in the room can smell the sweet scent of her arousal.

Axel stands from the table abruptly. "Thank you for dinner," he says, turning on his heel. "I'll see myself out."

I nod at Ethan, who scoots his chair back from the table, blocking his path.

"Well, now, don't be too hasty," my brother says, an edge of taunting in his voice. "We couldn't let a guest leave without showing our hospitality. And you wouldn't want to be rude and run out on us now, would you?"

Axel's jaw grinds back and forth.

"That's right," I say. "If you're offering to share, I think you should know the full meaning of the word."

"I understand I hurt Luna, and I've tried to make amends," Axel says.

"I don't think you do understand, mongrel," I say. "*We're* the ones who sat with Luna and consoled her after you threw her away. You didn't see it, so how can you understand? *We* rescued her and nursed her back to health. When she got hurt again running from *your* captivity, who saved her? I did. We took turns taking care of her, hoping like hell she didn't die. If you want to see why she didn't choose you, Axel, come on back to the bedroom and you can see for yourself just how good we take care of her."

The bastard's face goes a mottled gray, as if he's swamped with shame.

"Yes, you haven't seen any of the bedrooms since I fixed them up," Luna says, hopping to her feet and clapping her hands, obviously relieved to distract us from the tension. "Let's go see them."

She grabs Axel's hand and drags him down the hall. I glance at my brothers and grin. "Want to help me make his head spin like a fucking demon?" I ask. "Because I had to watch him fuck her in the woods and not do shit about it, so he's going to get to do the same tonight. But this time, we'll show him what sharing a mate is supposed to look like."

"I'll make sure he stays and watches," Ethan says.

I give him a funny look—I've never known Ethan to turn down pussy, and Luna's not just any pussy. She's my mate, and I'm offering to share her. We've shared lots of women before, but we've never given a fuck about one, so this is different.

Callan nods, though, standing from the table. "Thank you."

When we reach the bedroom, Luna's inside pointing out the new lace curtains, and Axel's standing in the doorway, looking tense as fuck. I give him a hard shove, and he stumbles forward before spinning to face us.

"You're not going anywhere," I say. "Until you see what you gave up, and what it means to share the right way, not for some bullshit purposes."

Ethan grabs Axel and yanks his hands behind his back, and I scoop up Luna. She gives a little giggling shriek and slides her small, soft hand behind my neck. I kiss her hard as I make my way to the bed. If I kissed a woman before—and I'm not sure I have—it couldn't hold a candle to how it feels to savage Luna's delicious little mouth. To taste her, to plunge my tongue inside like I'm thrusting it into her sweet little pussy, is pure heaven.

I hear Axel growling out protests, but he doesn't use his dominance to force Ethan to release him. The sicko might be fighting it, but he wants to watch us wreck his tight little mate. If he really wanted to go, he could.

I lay Luna down on the bed, and Callan slides off her shirt and shorts, leaving her stretched out in nothing but a pair of purple silk panties, bought on Axel's dime.

Luna seems torn between breaking up the growling match going on between Axel and Ethan, and submitting to the pleasure we're offering. I use a little of my own dominance to urge her to forget about the others, and she melts back on the bed with a sigh when Callan starts kissing her, massaging her tits and pulling at her nipples while he devours her mouth.

I spread her legs and have my way with her pussy, lapping at her like a man who's been withheld food for far too long. She moans and lifts her hips, and I force two long fingers into her tight core at once. She squeals, but I know she can take it. I pump into her while I suck and nip at her clit. She moans and writhes beneath my mouth, her juices slicking my fingers.

"Want to do that to me?" Callan growls to her, nipping at her ear.

"What?" she asks, her voice breathless.

"Want to suck my cock?"

She nods eagerly, and Callan straddles her torso, props her head on three pillows, and thrusts his cock into her mouth. I hear her gagging, and I just about come in my pants. Instead, I add another finger, working it past her stretched entrance.

Her moans grow louder as she's sucking my brother while he pumps into her mouth from above. I eat her cunt until she comes, crying out around Callan's cock.

He pulls out of her mouth and grabs his cock, aiming at her face. Cum rains down over her face and throat, and he slides back to unload the last of it over her creamy tits with their rosebud nipples.

She's panting, crying, moaning, and bucking into my mouth. Her hands fist the sheets and tear at the bedspread as I suck her clit hard until she comes a second time.

"Too much, Warrick!" Luna cries. "I can't take anymore."

Grinning, I withdraw from her, pulling my slick fingers from her juicy core. "Oh, I'm just getting started, baby girl," I say, standing and unzipping my jeans. "Now I'm going to fuck your cunt until you scream."

I glance back at Ethan, who's wrestling with Axel. I grin at the Alpha as I knock his mate's quivering thighs apart and lower my enormous cock to her little pink pussy. I'm about to wreck her, and he knows it. He knows he can't compete with me. The minute my brother lets him go, he'll slink away like a beaten Omega, knowing he's no match for us.

"Daddy, please," Luna whimpers, drawing my attention back to her.

At the sound of her sweet words, my cock throbs precum onto her waiting flesh. I turn back to my sexy little mate, forgetting all about our audience. Throwing her legs over my shoulders, I force my cock deep inside her. She shrieks and bucks, tears of strain trickling from the corners of her eyes as she takes every inch of me. I ravage her tight little cunt, relishing every cry I tear from her lips as I demolish her until she comes, screaming my name.

When I'm done with her, I turn to see my brothers watching with hungry eyes. Axel is long gone.

# Chapter Nineteen

*Luna*

I'm yanked from the fog of bliss at the sound of the front door slamming shut. I can feel Axel's wolf, how wounded it is, and guilt cloaks me like a shroud. I didn't mean for this to happen, even though some part of me thought Axel deserved to see what he threw away. That's why I let him stay and watch.

"Go make sure he doesn't destroy shit," Warrick says to Ethan.

Ethan leaves the room. I know Axel wouldn't destroy my house, though. At least I hope he wouldn't. He did demolish our swamp home, according to Evan. But I don't trust vampires, so I'm not sure if that's true.

The light of a half-moon streams through the slit in my blue and white lace curtains, lighting up the bed.

Callan lays on one side of me, playing with my nipples and stroking my breast.

Warrick gives a low growl and settles in on my other side. "Did my baby girl like that?" he asks.

"So much," I say, snuggling in beside him.

"You want me to share you with Ethan, too?" he asks.

"Yes, please," I say, squirming at the thought of what Axel interrupted earlier.

He chuckles and gives my nipple a tweak. "Wouldn't Axel shit himself if we turned you into a regular club whore?"

"What's that?" I ask.

He rolls onto his side to face me. "What we like to do to them," he says, running his calloused fingers up my side, making me shiver. "Is one of us wrecks their cunt while another fucks them in the ass. Sometimes the third one fucks their face at the same time. Then we switch around. Keep going all night until they're overflowing with cum."

"Oh," I whisper. "I'd like that."

Warrick laughs quietly, a sound I don't think I've heard before. "You're a regular little slut, aren't you?" he asks, sliding his hand between my thighs. "You'd do anything for an orgasm."

"Why wouldn't I?" I ask. "It's the best feeling ever."

"Can't argue with that," he agrees, sinking a finger into me.

Callan clears his throat and gives me a significant look, and I'm pretty sure I know what the wants. I thread my fingers through Warrick's chest hair and look up at him through my lashes.

"So, actually, I was thinking…" I begin. "Maybe I'd like to be mates with all three of you all the time."

"Is that right?" Warrick asks, pumping into me until I almost lose my head.

"Yes," I said, closing my eyes and sinking into the pleasure.

"Well," he says. "I don't guess I mind sharing, as long as it's with my brothers. I've done it plenty before."

"Thank you," I say, leaning in to kiss him before giving in to his skillful fingers and letting him shoot me into the stars again.

Later, Warrick falls asleep on one side of me, and Callan snuggles close on the other. I should be perfectly and truly content now that we've cleared up the mate situation. But I can feel Axel's wolf all the way from down the street, can feel the anguish I caused.

A fat tear spills from my eye.

"What's wrong?" Callan asks, propping himself up on one elbow. "Why are you crying?" He leans down and sucks the tears from my face, waking Warrick.

Warrick clears his throat and says in a groggy voice, "Do we have a problem?"

"We hurt Axel," I sob.

"*We* didn't hurt Axel—Axel hurt Axel," Warrick says, wrapping a protective arm around me. "Breaking a sacred oath the way he did is inexcusable."

"Yes, but hasn't he suffered enough?" I reach for the sheet to wipe my eyes.

"Not hardly, Luna," Callan says. "I don't think you understand the enormity of his actions. No one breaks the sacred True Mate bond. Some wolves actually die from it, when their mate dies or is killed. Or they lose their minds, like your mama did. Axel did that to you knowing that could be the consequence. He's getting off easy."

"I doubt he sees it that way," I say in a too-small voice.

"Callan's right, baby girl," Warrick murmurs sleepily. "At your request, I spared his life. But that don't mean he doesn't deserve to die."

"You're tender hearted, and we love you for it," Callan says to me. "Now put him out of your mind and be here with us."

Warrick sighs again, and after a minute, he resumes snoring.

Callan lowers himself back to prone and nuzzles my neck. I smile and pretend to be okay for his sake, stroking his chest and playing with his unruly hair until he falls asleep. But I lay there half the night, feeling as battered as I did when I woke up from my wolf attack coma.

The next day, Callan and Warrick are already gone when I drag myself from bed. My heart feels as heavy as the stones lining the creek near their house. I pad to the kitchen and find a note resting on the table, scrawled in Callan's messy handwriting.

*Gone hunting. See you tonight.*

In a way, I'm glad. I don't want them around when Axel stops by today to bring me gifts or ask if I need anything. I intend to explain that I didn't mean to hurt his wolf and telling him how sorry I am.

I make breakfast and sit at the window seat, waiting for him to come knocking.

But I finish breakfast, and he's not there. I wash up and then tend the garden out back, looking up whenever someone strolls by. None of them are Axel.

All day, he never comes.

Nor does he stop by that night. Or the next day…or the day after that. *Or* the five days following.

Finally, I see him driving his truck down the street one day. My wolf leaps with joy. He's okay after all!

I race out onto the sidewalk, waving wildly, but his truck lumbers past without slowing.

I'm sitting at the counter the next morning when Callan comes whistling in. "What's up?" he asks, setting the coffee on. "You're looking morose for a girl who just got fucked until she couldn't take it no more."

I manage a small smile. "What's morose?"

"That," he says, gesturing to my face before taking a seat beside me. "What's bothering you, pet?"

"I miss the coffee Axel used to bring," I admit.

"Oh, now, don't you worry about that," he says, tucking my lilac hair behind my ear. "How about this? I'll take you down there right now, and you can get whatever frou-frou coffee shit you want."

"Okay," I say, nodding because I know he doesn't really mean shit. He said that's just a word to describe things in general.

I hop on his bike with him, and we race along the streets of Jacksonville, under the heavy sky. The air smells restless again. At the coffee shop, we step inside, and my wolf leaps high inside me, threatening to take me over. Our eyes fix on the blond-haired man at the counter—Axel. He takes his coffee and turns, his blue eyes landing on me. Without a word, his jaw tightens, and he pivots and heads out a side door.

A blade of regret cuts through my muscles and bones, leaving me raw and bloody. I should never have made him stay and see that I'm someone else's mate. His wolf will never believe it.

The coffee doesn't even taste good, even though it's filled with cream and all the flavors of syrup that I want. I only drink half of it before I ask Callan to take me home.

The next week passes the same way. I'm happy that the brothers are sharing me, that there's no secrets between us. We're our own little family, closer than ever. We eat together every night. We joke around as usual. During the day, they head out and do whatever boys do. At night, I fuck Warrick and sometimes Callan, too. It feels as good as it always did, but something's different.

Sometimes they ask me if I want to go out somewhere, but I politely decline. I need to stay close in case Axel stops by, and to guard my house. My wolf feels strangely, jealously possessive of it, even though no one has tried to mess it up, and Axel hasn't said he wants it back.

When another week has passed with no sign of Axel, I can hardly stand it.

Warrick tromps in one morning and says, "We're going hunting for deer today. Real deer, not those puny Key deer. Why don't you come with us, Luna? It'd be good for you to get out and hunt."

"Yeah, come with us," Ethan says, winding his arms around me. "It's a blast to take down a big deer. And I'm in the mood for venison."

"That sounds nice," I admit. "But I might stay in one more day."

"You gotta let Axel go, pup," he says, ruffling the top of my head. "It's for the best. He finally got the message and is leaving you to live your life on your terms. Just like you wanted."

"Maybe," I say, adding a sad smile. "Or maybe I crushed his heart."

"More like his ego," Callan says. "An Alpha's got a lot of pride, and you shoved a red-hot poker right up the ass of it. He ain't comin' around here after that."

The realization of how much I miss Axel bobs to the surface.

"But I *liked* having him around," I cry.

Warrick shakes his head and strides toward the front door. "A little late for that, baby girl," he calls back. "Now come and hunt with us and take your mind off it."

But my wolf refuses to come out. She's as mad at me as Axel must be.

A few minutes later, the guys get tired of trying to convince me, and they take off on their own. Three motorcycle engines roar and zoom off down the street, and I sit in the stew of misery I cooked up for myself. But I'm tired of moping and dwelling in that misery, so I decide to pull up my big girl britches and do something about it. I put on my shoes and head over to confront Axel. Enough's enough.

As I stride up the sidewalk toward his house, a gusty wind whips my hair in a tangle around my head. The palm trees sway back and forth with a backdrop of dark clouds. A storm that's been taking its time in arriving has finally decided to make its presence known.

Seagulls struggle for purchase in the airwaves overhead. I feel sorry for birds when the weather's bad—their delicate wings can't compete with gale-force winds. Even I have to put my head down and force my way up the street. When I arrive at Axel's house, I'm completely winded.

I stride up his porch stairs and rap on the front door. After a minute, he opens up. When he sees me, his expression becomes dead and lifeless.

"Hey, Axel," I say, my heart hammering in my chest.

"Hey, Luna," he says, his voice cool. "Help you?"

My wolf whines at his cold treatment. I chew on my lip before saying, "Can I come in? I need to talk to you."

"Suit yourself," he says. "But I don't have much time, so make it quick."

He moves away from the door and disappears into the house.

I enter but stand stiffly just inside the door.

A pile of puffy orange things that look like small pants filled with foam sits on the floor next to the sofa. Axel taps away at his phone. Then, he holds it up to his ear and says, "Hey. Do you have the supplies I asked you to get?... Great. Meet me at Adolfa's house. She'll be our coordinator... Uh-huh... Yeah... Okay. See you there."

"Who was that?" I ask when he sets down the phone.

"My Second in Command."

He could have just said Ama. Or he could have just walked over and punched me in the gut because that's what I feel at the friendly tone he used with her and the wooden voice he's using with me.

"What are you and Ama doing?" I can't keep the jealousy from my voice.

"Working to keep our pack safe. A hurricane's coming, and we're responsible for the entire pack's safety." He moves about his kitchen, opening doors, retrieving items, and tossing them into boxes.

"You think it's a hurricane?"

"I know it is. Now, what did you want to talk about?" He strides toward the pile of orange things, scoops them up, and heads outside.

I follow him. "What are those?"

"Life jackets."

The wind pushes us down the walkway from his house. Axel dumps the whole pile in his truck bed and heads back inside, with me continuing to follow.

"Anything I can do to help?" I say, grabbing the screen door before it whacks me in the head.

"Nope." He strides down the hall, opens a hall closet, and retrieves several lanterns and a box that says "flashlights" on the side.

"Are you sure?" I ask hopefully. "What do you need done? I can carry things even if I don't know what they are. I won't ask you questions and slow you down."

"Don't worry about it," he says. "Ama's helping. That's her job. We've got it covered."

Another stab of jealousy tears at my stomach. I could have been his Second, but I chose the triplets instead. "I see."

"Do you?" he says, finally looking at me with a world of hurt in his eyes.

It makes my wolf twist up tight inside me with her head and tail down. "Can I just explain what happened that night?" I ask, my tone pleading.

"I know exactly what happened," he growls. "Though I'm trying my damnedest to forget it by any means necessary."

I race to catch up with him. "What does that mean?"

"You made it real fucking clear that you can do whatever you want with whomever you want," he says, opening the cab and placing the lanterns inside. "That street goes two ways, Luna."

"What street?" I ask, misery and confusion rising inside me.

"I don't have time for this," he says, rounding the bumper and heading toward the driver's side.

"You're leaving?" I call over the howling wind.

"I told you. There's another goddamned hurricane coming. It's my job to keep the pack safe—a job you rejected. Good thing Ama's stepping up, like she always does."

If I hear her name one more time, I'm going to bleed to death, right here on the sidewalk.

"Let me come and help you. I can explain everything in the truck."

He gives me a sour look. "You made yourself perfectly clear, Luna."

He opens the driver's side door and clambers inside. I race around the truck and grab the handle before he can slam it shut. "Wait!"

He huffs out a sigh. "Let go of my door, Luna."

"I don't want to. I want you to stay and let me explain. Or let me come with you. I—I'll make it up to you. I was stupid and hurting and wrong, and I don't know how to do this thing people call relationships. I'm sorry."

His mouth bunches up and scoots to one side. "It's for the best, Luna," he finally says in a flat tone. "Let it go and move on. I did. You can, too. I want you to be happy, and clearly, you can't be happy with me. So, go be happy with them."

Angry tears track down my cheeks. "You can't mean that."

"I can, and I do. You made it clear who's important to you, and it isn't me." His expression softens, no longer the carved granite of a minute ago. "Now, please let go of my truck. My pack needs me."

"You mean they need you and Ama," I wail.

He sighs. "Head inside and put your house on the list for weatherproofing. We're doing all we can before the hurricane arrives. That way we won't lose as many homes."

I step away from his truck and stand there as he drives away without a backwards glance. What have I done? I suddenly wish the triplets had never found me.

# Chapter Twenty

*Ethan*

The wild winds have already begun testing the roof's mettle, so after the hunt, I start gathering my tools to work on it. This storm's going to be a bitch. The clouds look like bloated cows, and every body of water has white-capped waves. Mother Nature's serving us up one whale of a weather front—for the millionth time this decade. We just can't catch a break around these parts.

"What are you doing?" Luna asks, watching me as I buckle on my tool belt.

"Gonna go make sure your pretty little house doesn't flood," I say, smiling down at her. "Secure the shingles and add shutters to the windows."

"Can I come?"

I open my mouth to say no, she'll ask too many questions and slow me down. But she stares up at me with her big pretty eyes, and my resolve crumbles. I just can't take it when she fixes me with those purple doe eyes. I can't bring myself to deny her anything her sweet little heart desires.

"Sure, pup," I say. "Come on up with me."

None of us can seem to get her out of the house, so this will be a good chance for her to do something normal, though I figure I'll spend as much time explaining how to use the hammer as actually swinging it. She's been keeping to herself a lot since the night we forced Axel to watch my brothers fuck her. That asshole deserved every ounce of pain he experienced for hurting our Luna, but we agreed amongst ourselves to let Luna have her space to process the experience. You can't force insight or wisdom.

We climb a ladder and pad onto the roof. Luna crouches to examine the shingle, nodding to herself. She finds a loose one and pulls it up, peeking under at the lone nail remaining. Then she gets a handful of nails and a hammer and gets busy. As she straddles the roof with me, she seems to have let go of some burden. She's still quiet, but she doesn't look sad. She's just concentrating. And damned if she can't wield a mean hammer, no explaining necessary on my part.

She pounds nails into the shingles that we bought to mend the ones that were clinging to the roof by a thread, and damn but she looks sexy. The wind billows around her, blowing out her long, lilac locks and plastering her sleeveless top against her body. The lack of sleeves shows off the muscles in her arms, and I'll be damned if they aren't the sexiest thing I've ever seen, in part because this is the last thing I expected when we came up here.

Luna seems so fragile because of the state we found her in, and so innocent because of her lack of social skills, but I have to remind myself she's not weak by any means. She may be submissive and adorably clueless, but she's strong and capable. After all, she was taking care of her mother for years, surviving on her own and being responsible for another's survival on top of it. She's a strong ass woman who deserves every ounce of respect I've got to give.

She looks up from the nail she just secured in the shingles and smiles at me. "What are you looking at?"

"What do you think?"

I'm pleased to see a genuine smile on her face—not the fake ones she's been giving us lately. My brothers and I might be rough around the edges, but we all know when a woman is faking it.

"I think you're looking at me," she says, still smiling.

"You're right. You win the prize."

"What's the prize?" she asks, cocking her head to the side.

I tap my lips with my fingertip.

"I won a kiss?"

"Come over here and see," I tease.

She gets on her hands and knees and crawls along the ridge of the roof toward me. I sit back, ready for her kiss. When she reaches me, though, she lowers her head and gently bites the fly of my zipper.

"What's that for?" I ask, loving the attention.

"It's for offering me a prize," she says, looking at me through her lashes.

"You don't have to repay a prize. Now come and get it while it's fresh."

She stretches her neck and puckers her pretty mouth.

I tip her chin up with one finger and gift her with the softest kiss I've ever given. With Luna, there are endless firsts.

When she pulls away, she gives a little sigh of pleasure. "That was a good prize."

"There are more where that came from," I say, patting my knee.

She slides up onto my lap, her little body curling into mine as her delicate arms circle my neck. "I'm sorry I've been so weird lately," she says, watching me from under her lashes.

"Don't worry about it, pup. You've been through a lot. Your wolf spirit is so strong, though—that's what I was thinking about when I was watching you. Not many people could endure what you've been through and come out of it with half the grace and gentleness you have." I attempt to smooth her hair away from her face, but I know I'm in competition with the damned wind.

"That's nice," she says, nuzzling her cheek into my palm.

"No one's ever called me nice before you," I say with a grin, shaking my head.

"I have a question about that," she says, cocking her head. "Why not?"

"And I have an answer," I say, sliding my hands around her back. "Because I'm not."

"I think you are," she says. "But I have another question."

"Shoot."

This probably isn't the safest place to hang out during a storm, but I know we've got a bit before the real fun starts. And I'm not going to waste the chance and risk putting her back into her gloomy funk.

She toys with the front of my T-shirt. "The night… You know… When Axel… *That night.*" Her lips pinch together.

"What about it?" Pushing my hands beneath her shirt, I stroke her back.

"Why didn't you...." She nibbles her lip. "Why didn't you let Axel leave?"

"My job was to make the bastard watch and suffer," I say. "See what he gave up, and how much better off you are with us. We see you for what you are, and he never did. You're a fucking treasure, Luna. He deserved to be tormented by seeing other men give you pleasure when he threw away that chance."

"What about you?" she asks.

"What about me?" I ask, leaning away a bit.

"You had to see that, too," she says. "Were you tormented, too?"

She peers up at me shyly, like she actually has doubts about that.

"Yeah, pup," I say quietly, raising my gaze to the sky. "I was. And I reckon I deserved it, too."

Her eyebrows raise and her eyes widen. "Why? Did you reject a True Mate, too?"

"No, pup. Nobody in his right mind would do that. I know you think different, but I've never been a nice man when it comes to women. I fuck 'em once, and then I'm done. I don't care if they've got feelings or if I hurt 'em. They don't matter to me. They're not True Mates, but I toss them the way Axel did you, like they're trash."

"You've always been good to me," she says, her face furrowed.

"You bring out the best in people."

"No, I don't. Just look at Axel."

"Fuck Axel. That dumb son of a bitch should be castrated so he can't have brainless offspring to follow in his footsteps."

We sit in silence for a minute, and I try to ignore the weight and heat of Luna's body in my lap. "Have you always been mean?" she asks after a while.

"Nah, not always," I say. "I thought I loved a woman once—the first woman I ever fucked. But I was just a pup like you—even younger. I didn't know better."

"Better than what?"

"I must've been sixteen, and she was twenty-four, twenty-five."

"So?" Luna says. "I'm eighteen, and you guys are twice my age."

"But it's different with you." I bunch her flying hair in my hand and hold it behind her head.

"How so?" she asks, staring up at me with open curiosity.

"I don't know." I shrug. "It just is. You're fucking irresistible."

I like how with her, there's no games. She doesn't know to play coy, to hide what she truly wants and pretend to be what someone else wants until she has him reeled in. She's just herself, our luscious little Luna, and that's a thousand times more enticing than any put-on air.

"What happened with the older woman?" Luna asks.

"I don't really want to talk about that." I squirm beneath her, pushing my cock up against her bottom, hoping it distracts her. She's a little pleasure chaser, and I already know my brothers placate her with orgasms.

But maybe she's catching on, because she narrows her eyes. "I want to talk about it," she says.

I sigh. "We fucked for a while, and I caught feelings. She was this hot, experienced, older woman, and I felt like a million bucks that I landed her. Made me think I was in love and shit."

I shake my head, trying to get the bitter taste of memory out of my mouth.

"What happened?

"I made the mistake of telling her how I felt, and she laughed her ass off. Said she needed a real man, not a kid. Someone who could take care of her, not just fuck her senseless every night. Said she was just having a little fun with me, but it was nothing serious."

"Isn't fun a good thing, though?"

"Not if you want more than that," I say. "I was fucking humiliated, but that's neither here nor there. I learned my lesson, though. I never let a woman get to me again. I've fucked around plenty, and I made sure to get out early so it don't mean shit. If they think it does, that's their problem. I just think they're pathetic for caring about a man like me and thinking it could be more."

"So… It can't be more?" she asks. "Not for you, anyway."

"No, pup," I say, circling my arm around her little body. "That's not what I'm saying. With you, I *want* it to be meaningful. I've had threesomes and gangbangs with my brothers before. They're fun as fuck. But I didn't want our first time together to be that way because… Well, for the first time in my fucking life, I think I do want it to mean something to the woman. To you."

I squeeze her hip and search her beautiful eyes.

"Oh, Ethan," she says, laying her small hand on my bearded cheek. "You make me feel more special than anyone in the world."

"You… You mean a lot to me, pup," I say. "Even if I didn't fuck you. That don't mean I didn't want to. I just want to… Deserve you."

"You do," she says, her eyes shiny like she might cry. "I love you, Ethan. I love all of you."

No one's ever said that to me before, and it lands heavy and immovable on my heart. It's a heavy burden, but one I'll work every day of my life to bear, to be worthy of the love of this little wolf angel who blew into our lives like a hurricane and tumbled us all head over tail.

I pull her in, cradling her soft little body against my hard one as I kiss her good and long. She shifts her position, straddling my hips and grinding against me while we kiss more. After a while, even with the whipping wind, I can smell how wet she is.

"Luna," I say, tearing my mouth from hers when I can't take it anymore. "You gotta stop or I won't be able to help myself."

"Help yourself from what?"

"I won't be able to hold back from fucking you silly."

The tip of her tongue lands on her upper lip, and she reaches for my fly. She frees my cock with her deft fingers, running her little hand up and down my thick shaft until I think I'll come then and there. "That's not helping," I growl. "You better stop if you don't want to get that pussy pounded and that belly filled with my seed."

"What if I do?" she asks, a flirty little smile on her lips.

"Then slide those jeans down, pup, because I'm about to breed you so deep I give you pups even if it's not your heat." I grab her around the waist and flip her over, rolling on top of her and parting her thighs.

Her eyes widen. "Is that possible?"

"I guess we'll find out."

I push down her jeans and slide a finger through her slick cunt. She moans and shivers, and I grab my cock and push it against her entrance. The stretch of her tightness makes precum ooze from my tip and into her straining opening. She rocks up against me, and I push my hips forward, forcing my tip inside her. She gasps, her fingers gripping my arms, her eyes going wide. I give her a few seconds to relax and adjust before bracing myself on my hands and sinking my cock slowly into her. Her cunt grips me in its stranglehold, and her mouth falls open, a little stitch pulling between her eyebrows when the head of my cock nudges her cervix.

"Oh, my fucking God," I breathe, resting my forehead on hers. "I'm going to breed you so full of my babies, pup. I want to put a million of them inside your belly right now."

She pants through the pain until she's adjusted, and then I begin to pump my full length into her slick little pussy. Right here on the roof, in front of the devil and everyone, I proceed to give her all my love. The weather goddess spills her tempest across the land, heedless of our actions. And like the storm that's about to unload on us, everything I've held back through the years comes bursting up, washing over her, over me.

"I love you, Luna. I fucking love you."

The words spill from my lips unbidden, but I wouldn't take them back for anything.

"I love you, Ethan," she cries, bucking her narrow hips under mine. When she wraps her little legs around me and comes on my cock, my name on her lips and her cunt squeezing me in its hot, wet little vice, I come harder than I've ever come in my life.

# Chapter Twenty-One

*Luna*

The tempest is on its way, and I think it's going to tear me from everyone and everything, just like in my dream. The winds are howling, screaming through the rafters, whistling through the telephone poles. Axel hasn't stopped by to make sure we're safe, even though I put my name on his list like he asked. He's supposed to tell us where to go if things get worse. We're not safe—we never even got the shutters on. The triplets are frantically trying to get them up before the worst of it hits.

While they're busy, I decide to run back to Axel's and get the emergency plan myself, since he was too mad to bring it to me. Head down, raincoat wrapped around my body and tied securely at the waist, I power through the wind that nearly takes me off my feet. When I get to his porch, I have to pry open the screen door with both hands. I don't bother knocking, just hurl myself inside and release the door, afraid it'll knock me out if it hits me.

"Axel? That you?" comes a dreaded, familiar voice. Then Ama saunters down the hall, her arms full of clothes.

"Not Axel," I say, eyeing her.

"Oh," she says, wrinkling her nose like I still smell the way I did the day she found me in the swamp. "Just you. Want to help me fold this laundry?"

The smug smile on her face puts me on guard. "Why are you doing your laundry here?"

She grins. "Not mine. *Ours.* He's out making sure everyone's house is storm proof and they know where to go if things get dicey. He's so considerate that way." She drops the armload of clothes onto the sofa, revealing that she's not wearing anything. "He and I will ride out the storm together."

My irritation kicks up a notch. "I just came for the emergency plan."

"Sure you don't want to help?" She plucks a pair of boxers out of the pile and holds them up for inspection, and a secretive smile flashes across her face. "Wait, never mind. You've helped enough."

"What does that mean?" I realize my fingers have curled into fists, so I shake them out.

"Well," Ama says, folding the boxers and setting them on the back of the sofa. Next, she plucks a lacy bra from the pile and again makes that sly smile. "Thanks to your stupidity—he would have given you the world, you know... Anyway, you did the job I couldn't figure out how to do. I guess I should actually thank you."

She grins and arches her eyebrows.

"What job?" I ask, confusion and a bad feeling welling up inside. My heart pounds as loud as the wind outside, and my mouth is suddenly parched. "Being his Second?"

Ama titters and places the bra beside the boxers, giving it a little pat. "I've been doing plenty of *jobs*, if you catch my drift. Mmm...he's yummy. So big."

Her tone makes wires inside me start to fray even though I don't entirely know what she's talking about. "What job did I do?" I demand, more loudly this time.

"You sent him straight into my arms, of course," she says, her voice matter-of-fact as she continues folding their mixed laundry. "Before, he was always resistant, giving a hundred reasons why we shouldn't be together. But a man with a wounded pride, he's vulnerable, isn't he? And I have you to thank for that. I got everything I ever wanted thanks to you. When he was too hurt to know what to do with himself, I was there to lick his wounds, to make him feel like a big man again."

"He is a big man," I manage, my voice small. She isn't saying what I think she's saying... Is she?

"I know. And seeing him so beaten down and despondent, it just broke my heart." She picks up a pair of satiny panties that match the bra, folds them and places them on her growing stack of clothes. "Good thing I was there to comfort him and prove to him I was exactly what he needed all along. A strong, capable, experienced woman, not a dumb little puppy who doesn't know what a blowjob is."

Each item of co-mingled underwear slices the frayed nerves inside until I'm one giant nerve ending. "What is it?"

"Something you'll probably never do, pillow princess," she says with a sneer. "It's part of sex, in case you still hadn't figured it out. We're together now. The whole pack approves, since I'm already his Second. And since he needs a mate, as soon as I go into heat, he can breed me, and I'll give him the heirs he needs to be a fully-realized Alpha with the lineage to carry on the title. You'll be nothing but a distant memory... Or a nightmare that he wakes up to when he's lying safe in my arms."

My wolf is howling with such rage and hurt and betrayal inside me that I can't even think right now. I can't breathe, can't do anything except experience the most intense pain of my life, almost as bad as the mate bond severing. This must be what Axel felt when he was forced to watch me, only his pain was one hundred times worse because he had to watch it and not just find out from someone else. He had to see it with his own eyes, knowing it was punishment for something he'd done and not just the unintended consequences of his mistake.

He did this *because of* me, but not *to* me. He moved on with his life, like he said, but he spared me the detail. I made him see every detail. I hurt him on purpose as revenge for the hurt he caused me. Oh, I'm a terrible, terrible person!

My lungs are heaving, but I can't tear my gaze away from the bitch who got my mate… The mate whose heart I crushed to smithereens.

The wind howls around the house, screeching like a demon. A loose shutter bangs against the siding, making a whack, whack, whack kind of racket—it matches the erratic beating of my heart. I finally manage to pry my feet from the floor and turn to run.

"Not so fast," Ama snarls, leaping in front of me and blocking my exit. Her face is a horrible mask of rage as she seizes my arm.

"Let me go!" I cry, trying to pry her fingernails from my arm.

"Not happening. That wolf I sent to kill you failed to do his job, so I'm going to finish it."

"You sent that wolf to kill me?" My eyes open wide in shock. "That was *your* doing?"

"Of course it was, dimwit. Do you think random male wolves give a shit about you? I paid him well, but the bastard didn't deliver. He was supposed to get rid of you for good so Axel would run into my arms. Fuck was I pissed when you rolled back into town."

"He'd never have anything to do with you if he knew what kind of person you are," I shout, spitting at her and trying to pull free of her grip.

"How fortunate that you showed up today, when he's busy helping the wolves who are actually deserving," she says, almost cheerfully. "But you're right—as long as you're around, he might never really give up on you. And I can't risk losing the Alpha now that I've gotten him at last." Her eyes are wild, as wild as the storm billowing outside the door.

I wrench my arm out of her grasp at last, raising my palms toward her. "Okay, you can have him. I lost. I don't even want Axel. Just let me go, and I'll never see you again, I promise. I'll disappear with the triplets."

I try to sidle around her to get to the door, but she shoves me backward. "You're not going anywhere."

"I'm not?" I manage to squeak. "What are you going to do to stop me?"

"My god, you're dumb." A grin forms on her face, but she's an ugly person under the surface beauty. Even I can see that. "What do you think I'm going to do? Obviously I'm going to kill you and dispose of you in the rising water. What else would I do?"

I swallow hard, my heart racing as I meet her cold, evil eyes. She really means it. I'm about to die.

# Chapter Twenty-Two

*Axel*

Something is wrong. I can feel it somehow, even though Luna hasn't sworn into the pack, so we don't share the pack bond. But we still share some other bond, a curse that ties me to her no matter how much I deny it. My wolf frets inside me, sure that something is not right.

I sigh and try to focus again, piling sandbags along the edge of Kato's backyard to keep the water at bay. Luna finally got it through my thick head that she's with them now, not me. She wants nothing to do with me. She's got three thugs protecting her, and even though they're worthless wastes of wolf skin, they're not going to let anyone touch her. They'd rip anyone's head off who tried. It's a miracle they put up with me as long as they did. If I'd understood how things were, I would have walked away before. But I listened to my wolf, and I sure as fuck suffered enough for it. I don't need to go running to her house now. I never want to set foot in that place again.

But the little voice in the back of my mind keeps telling me something's wrong.

I reach through the bond I share with Ama.

*Ama, can you check on Luna? I haven't made it to a few houses at that end of the street. Stuck at Carina and Kato's a few more minutes.*

*Sure thing, boss. I knew you hadn't, and I took care of the last houses. Teamwork. Right, baby?*

*Thanks.*

I should be relieved, but something still doesn't feel right. After a few minutes, I reach through again.

*Did you see Luna?*

*Yes. She's fine.*

Despite her reassurance, I can't concentrate. I can feel something's amiss, and even though Ama talked to me, she had her shields up, preventing me from exploring her thoughts at all. I only got words, and words are cheap.

All wolves can protect their privacy, and ordinarily, I wouldn't question it. But when it involves Luna…

The nagging thoughts about Luna's well-being persist. I still trust my wolf intuition, and what my intuition tells me right now is that Ama is lying, and Luna is in trouble.

I can't fight the unease any longer—I've got to check on her. I call out to Kato and Carina, who are slinging sandbags down the line, and then I hit the road.

The windshield wipers are useless as I power up the street, which is already doused with a half-foot of water. It's only going to get worse. Palm trees are bent double, as if their trunks are made of putty, and a piece of flying tin narrowly misses the truck as I power through the storm.

When I get to Luna's, I leap out of the front seat and race up the walkway to her house. Pounding on the door yields nothing. Opening the door and yelling for Luna, for anyone, is equally fruitless. Is she out with her biker outlaws? Where would they possibly go in this storm?

I head back to the truck and drive as quickly as possible, given the wind and the rain slamming against my vehicle. I skid to a stop in front of my house. The driver's side door, caught in a sudden gust, nearly rips from its hinges as I throw it open. I race inside, my wolf on full alert. Something is wrong *here*.

I burst through the front door to see Ama holding Luna's body pinned to the floor, a knife pressed to her throat. Both women are bloody and banged up like they've been duking it out for a while. Ama's more muscular, and she's used it to her advantage, straddling Luna's back and gripping her hair with one hand, holding the blade with the other.

My wolf explodes out of me so fast my clothes are torn to shreds, pieces of fabric flying across the room.

"I'm doing this for us," Ama shrieks. "So nothing will come between us again!"

*Fuck that. We were never together in the first place.*

Getting our physical needs met and joining in a partnership are two separate things. As usual, Ama has skewed the facts.

Fangs bared, I leap, claws poised to take Ama down. My teeth land on the arm wielding the knife, and Ama screams, shifting into her wolf skin. I rip her front leg away from Luna, and the knife clatters to the ground. Luna rolls away, taking herself out of harm's way instead of trying to help and becoming a distraction or a liability.

*Smart girl.*

Ama cries out as I crunch down on her bone, grinding through muscle and tendon and snapping the bone. She snarls and snaps at me, trying to gain purchase on my neck. But she's diminutive compared to me, no match for her Alpha. She betrayed me—worse, she hurt my precious Luna. Without a second thought, I go for the kill strike, closing my teeth over her carotid artery and ripping out her throat. I drop her body to the floor and turn to Luna, blood dripping from my jaws.

I shift and scoop up my mate, who's huddling on the floor next to the sofa. Adrenaline pumps through me, and I feel like the king of the world, the most powerful wolf that's ever lived. I throw Luna down on the couch and dive on top of her, my mouth claiming hers roughly.

She gives a surprised little moan, her hands cupping my face and pulling me down, kissing me back with fierceness and desperation.

"I'm sorry," she pants out between kisses. "I'm sorry I ever chased you away. If I'd known you'd run to the arms of that vile woman, I'd never have let you go."

I draw her knees open and slide up between them, moaning when my bare cock rubs against the heat between her thighs. Every cell in my body aches with need.

"She's nothing," I say. "Just a hole to fill to pass the time."

"What about me?" Luna asks, grinding her hips up against mine.

"You're my mate, my *True Mate*, my everything," I say, reaching down and wrenching her jeans down so hard they tear like mine did when I shifted. I push a finger into her tight, slick little hole, and she whimpers with pleasure, biting at my lips, scratching my neck, and bucking against me.

"Then show me," she manages, dropping back on the couch.

"Oh, I'm about to," I say, grabbing my stiff cock and lowering it to her entrance.

"Did you fuck Ama here?" she asks, closing her knees around my hips.

"What does that matter?" I growl. "You let the triplets pass you around like a fucking whore."

"If she means so little to you, then show me," Luna shoots back. "Fuck me on her body." She thrusts her finger at the dead wolf across from us, lifeless next to the wall.

I draw back, shocked at her gruesome request. But my wolf roars with approval, wanting this primal need to be filled—victory and lust twist together into one urge as I snatch up Luna and carry her to the body of my Second. I killed Ama for her, and she's making me prove I don't regret it.

I don't. Not for a second.

I lay Luna down on the fur pelt of the wolf body. Its dark eyes are now clouded over like fog obscuring midnight, and she stares into the beyond. Luna takes a few sniffs and then rolls over onto her hands and knees. She looks over her shoulder at me, a wicked grin on her face. "I'll lick her blood," she says. "You fuck me."

The scent of her arousal is too intoxicating to let this moment pass. She sways her hips from side to side as she invites me to mate. I bend and run my tongue through her cunt, sweeping up and down her wet folds and tasting my mate, her scent made just for me. My wolf roars for me to claim her, and hers cries out in answer. I kneel up behind her as she lowers her head, lapping up the blood spreading across my hardwood floor.

The sight is enough to nearly make me wolf out again, but I hold him back as he howls to mark and claim our mate again. But I don't hesitate and go slow this time. She's no longer the scared little virgin I first claimed upstairs. She's a woman who's had multiple partners at once, one who knows what she wants. And her wolf says she wants to be plowed like a slut. I grip her narrow hips and thrust inside her, and she cries out. I answer by fucking her hard and rough, the dominating rhythm making her moan each time my hips hit her ass as I bury my cock to the hilt in her sweet, wet pussy.

She looks over her shoulder at me, her mouth streaked with gore, and I feel the knot swell at the base of my cock, the painful stretch as it enlarges. I flip over so Luna is on top, letting her ride me, her pale legs folded as she moves up and down. I watch the muscles in her ass flex and my cock sliding into her snug little hole until I can't bear it. Grabbing her leg, I swing it over me, turning her until she's facing me. Her eyes widen at the way my cock hits every place inside her. I slam up into her from below, loving the way she looks, so feral and bloody, a warrior who conquered her enemy.

Or at least I conquered her. Luna is my prize.

"Luna," I growl. "Fuck, I love you."

She leans down, wiping her hand in the blood before streaking it across my chest like a reminder of what I'd do for her. "That's right," she says. "You love me. Only me. Whose pussy do you belong inside?"

"Yours, Luna. Your pussy is mine, and I'm about to fucking destroy it."

"Yes," she moans. "And your cock is mine. All mine." Her possessiveness drives me to the edge, and I slam up into her as hard as I can. She squeals as I impale her, the knot stretching her until her eyes grow wide with alarm and she's gasping for relief. She rakes her nails down my chest in the throes of passion, drawing blood from my skin.

"So take all of it," I growl. "Even my knot. It's made for you." I pump into her harder, even when I hear the door open and feel the presence of other wolves. This is my claiming, and nothing but death will stop me. I slam into her until I think her fragile body will shatter with the force, but I don't let up. I thrust into her harder, stroking her slick core with my cock until her juices run down my balls and she writhes helplessly on top of me.

Her movements get wilder as she realizes she's pinned, that she can't move with the knot stretching her so good. I flip her over and grind deeper, filling her to the brim with every inch of me, watching her pant through the pain and pleasure to find her climax.

"Yes," she cries, her knees opening and closing, her hips grinding up against mine as I crush her down into Ama's body until I feel the wolf bones snapping beneath us. "Oh, yes! Come now, Axel. Breed me. Please!"

I wait until she's milking me, sucking me with her core in the throes of orgasm before I release inside her. My cum shoots into her, my wolf soul filling her with each wave of cum pouring into her tender center. I raise my head and roar with my wolf, and she howls with her own relief her legs wrapped around me and her body jerking with spasm of pleasure, her cunt stretched so tight it aches around the knot of my cock that's lodged insider her. Finally, she falls back in a whimpering heap of bliss, trembling all over as she submits to my claim in front of her three watching lovers.

# Chapter Twenty-Three

*Luna*

I'm still humming with the bliss of orgasm and the satisfaction my wolf feels at being claimed by Axel when I look up and see three hulking shapes standing in the doorway.

"Oh," I cry, scrambling up right on Ama's dead body.

Axel sucks in a breath, and I realize he's still knotted up inside me.

"What are you doing here?" I ask the triplets.

"We got worried about you," Ethan says. "We thought something might have happened to you."

"And now we can see that something did happen to you. *He* happened to you." Warrick steps through the doorway and charges toward us as if he's going to fight with Axel again. I wince when Axel pulls the swollen base of his cock from me, stepping in front of me to block Warrick's path.

"Wait," I cry, leaping to my feet and darting between the two men. "Axel saved my life."

Warrick halts, eyes the dead wolf, and then turns to us. His gaze sweeps my bruised, battered body, covered with bumps and scrapes. "What happened?" he demands.

"Ama tried to kill me," I say, rushing my words so he won't attack. "She wanted Axel and said I was in the way. She tried to kill me, but Axel killed her instead."

Warrick, Callan, and Ethan all turn to my Alpha, and their eyes shutter.

"I see," says Callan in a monotonous tone. His arms hang limply by his sides. Water drips from his fingertips, continuing its journey from his raincoat.

"When Ama said Axel was hers... I didn't like it," I admit. "I like that he defended me. I like having him around."

"So, you got back together with him," Ethan says, scowling.

"No, you don't understand. I like *all* of you." I hold out my hands, palms up, beseeching them. Something creamy and warm trickles down the inside of my thigh, tickling my skin.

Ethan's gaze drops to my legs, then Callan's, and then Warrick's. I shift side to side, uncomfortably. "Look," I say, trying to distract them. "Y'all know how lonely I was with Mama in the swamp. Now that I'm grown, I don't want that. We can all get along—make each other laugh and make each other dinner and sex each other. What's the harm in adding one more? Axel invited us all into the pack, and if we'd joined, he would have known I was in trouble from the start today. We can all be mates, can't we?"

Three sets of jaw drop open, and they stare at me like I've grown whiskers or horns in my cheeks.

"What are you saying?" Axel asks.

"I didn't like the fighting between these brothers, and I don't like it between you and them, either. I don't want to cause nobody pain. Let me make it up to you—all of y'all."

"How are you going to do that?" Callan asks.

"You have no idea what you're asking us to do, Luna," Warrick says, looking past me at Axel. "We've been hating this asshole for a fucking decade."

"And how's that working out for you?" I put my hands on my hips and try to swell up my chest like they do. It must work, because they all drop their gazes to my chest.

Callan lets out a snort, and the barest of smiles curves his lips.

I flash him a smile and then turn back to Warrick. "Who's it help to be at odds all the time? Axel said you could join the pack. He did his part. Now it's time for you to do what's best for your pack of three, too, Daddy."

"She has a point," Callan says.

I love him even more for his support.

"I don't know," Warrick says, scratching the back of his head. "Old grievances die hard."

A curious silence fills the room while outside, the storm rages on. Shutters slam against the window frames, the wind sings in the rafters, and rain pours and pours. I step toward the brothers, sidle between Callan and Ethan, and lace my fingers with theirs.

Warrick studies me with an indecipherable expression.

"Let's all accept each other and get along." I squeeze Callan's and Ethan's warm hands.

"Agreed," Axel says, straightening and managing to look imposing even though he's smaller than the other three and not wearing a stitch of clothes. "Let us let the destruction of Ama serve to herald a new day in the Jacksonville pack. And to remind everyone what happens when you hurt Luna."

He stares down the others, and for once, I understand. He's telling them they better do what I say, even though I'm the submissive wolf here. Because if they don't get along, that hurts me, and he'll hurt whoever does that. He'll do as I wish, and they better do it, too.

Ethan clears his throat. "Thanks for saving her life, man."

Callan grunts in agreement.

Warrick crosses his beefy arms over his chest.

"You've got to quit getting yourself into life and death messes," Callan says to me.

"I second that," Ethan says.

Warrick continues to shoot daggers at Axel with his eyes.

Axel ignores him.

"Come on, please?" I say, dropping the hands I've been holding and clinging to Warrick's beefy, tattooed bicep. "Let's just try it. If it doesn't work, we can try something else. What's the harm?"

"I'll try it," Ethan says behind me.

Warrick frowns at him.

"Count me in," Callan says. "I'm not losing Luna."

Warrick continues to glare.

"I'll do it on one condition," Axel says.

"Here we go," Warrick growls. "I was waiting for some negotiation coming from you, Alpha."

"I like to be predictable," Axel says coolly.

"What do you want?" Warrick demands.

"I want you," Axel says, matching Warrick's stance. "I need a new Second in Command, and I can think of no one finer."

I stand there blinking in surprise, and everyone else looks just as shocked.

"How much power will I hold?" Warrick says, scratching his scruffy neck.

"Second to only me," Axel says smoothly. "When I'm not here, whether dead or simply away, you're in charge." Axel appears calm and unruffled, and I admire him even more for it.

"Huh," Warrick says.

"Of course, the pack doesn't expect a dictator. That won't fly," Axel continues. "But you're a powerful man, Warrick. I believe you can guide with fairness and adherence to rules if given a chance."

"What do you think, Warrick?" I say, practically wriggling like a wolf pup.

He regards me, and his eyes soften. "Would that make you happy?" he asks gruffly.

"Would it ever!"

"I'll do it for you," he says. "If that's what you want, baby girl."

I'm practically glowing as I watch Warrick step toward Axel and shake his hand.

"I accept your offer, starting immediately," Warrick says.

"Thank you, Warrick," Axel says, giving his hand a firm shake. "It'll be an honor to rule the pack with you."

I whoop for joy, and Ethan picks me up and kisses me hard. I can't believe we finally did it. We're all united. Maybe we can all finally have what we want at last.

# **Chapter Twenty-Four**

*Luna*

Warrick, Ethan, Callan, Axel, and I sit around Axel's kitchen table, drinking beer and talking, trying to ignore the storm gathering strength outside and hoping it won't be a big one.

Warrick and Axel are already talking pack strategy, Axel filling in the new Second about pack laws. Even though Warrick can't officially start until we're sworn in, Axel sharing the details is a sign of trust that goes a long way. Instead of growling and snapping, Warrick is soaking it up like a sea sponge. It's good to see them working together instead of tearing at each other's throats.

Callan nudges me under the table with his feet, bringing my attention to him. He gives me a smile and a wink that makes my heart flip, then takes a swig of his beer. My whole belly fills up with warmth. Ethan squeezes my hand on the other side. I want to stay this way forever, but a loud banging on the front door interrupts.

"That doesn't sound good," Axel said, pushing up to his feet. "Must be an emergency for someone to leave their house in this."

As soon as he opens it, a male voice starts speaking like he's hopped up on six cups of coffee. I catch snatches of the conversation like, "...the baby is sick," and "water pouring in."

"Slow down, Borris. Take a breath. We'll be right there to help. Come in out of the rain while we get our weather gear on," Axel says calmly.

"You've got to hurry, man. My baby..." says Borris, a small, nervous-looking guy I vaguely recognize from around pack territory. His raincoat is sopping, and the hat on his head flops around his skull so he has to keep pushing it up.

"Borris, meet our new pack members, Warrick, Ethan, and Callan. And, you know Luna, right?"

Borris freezes in the foyer, eyeing the brothers like they're bog beasts. "Aren't they…?"

"Probably," Axel says, cutting him off. "But now they're allies, so let's get you some help."

"And she's the one you brought to the barbecue?" Borris says, looking utterly confused. "Your mate."

"Yes, that's her," Axel says after pulling on a raincoat. "Boys, let's go save Borris's baby. She and her mama are trapped, and they've got a leak flooding the house."

"On it," says Warrick, rising.

Callan and Ethan stand, too, heading for the closet where Axel is pulling out rain gear.

"There's a rowboat in the back, next to the shed. You go get it, Warrick. Callan and Ethan, gather some buckets from the shed. Luna, you'll be in the rowboat as we head to their house, down the street a few blocks. The boys and I will wade."

"But…" I protest, not wanting to be babied.

"No, buts. We need to keep you safe," Axel says, yanking on waders and heavy rubber boots. He tosses me one of the orange life vests I saw earlier. "Get that on, too."

"Just do it," Callan says, zipping up his raincoat. "You're important."

I flush with cozy feelings at their care. And I'm so damn proud of them for working together. But I hate to be treated like a wolf pup.

I hustle to get all my rain gear on, too.

And then we all exit into the howling storm.

The water's up to the men's knees as they wade down the street, and cars are pushed sideways on the road. The streetlights are still flickering intermittently. The men keep the rowboat steady as the wind whips spray across the top of the once-street, now more like an inlet.

I grip the sides of the rowboat with one hand and use the other hand to keep my hat on my head. The gusts want to whisk it away.

Finally, we reach Borris's house.

Warrick pulls the rowboat up to their front porch, where water sloshes between the cracks in the boards. He ties off the boat and helps me out of the rocking vessel onto the porch. "See? You still get to use your waders. We just can't have you drowning on us."

"Wife's in the dining room," Borris says, hurrying inside, babbling all the way. "The water pushed our credenza in front of the door. It's a heavy piece filled with dishes. Now it's jammed against the door. I tried to get her out. We had to board up the windows before the storm, or I would have helped her out the window."

"It's okay," Axel says, clapping him on the shoulder. "Shit happens in these storms, and this one is definitely stirring the shit."

As we clamber into the house, the electricity goes out, plunging us into near darkness.

"Shit," Warrick mutters.

"When it rains, it pours," Callan says.

"Anyone bring a light? A lantern? Anything?" Ethan says.

"Fuck," Axel mutters. "I gave them all out earlier, except for a couple I keep in my truck. Borris, can you get to yours?"

"It's, uh… It's in the dining room with my emergency light. At least my wife's got 'em."

I can practically hear the shame and regret dripping from his words.

We stumble in the dim interior, since the hurricane's made it nearly dark as night out, and the windows are boarded up. The baby's wails compete with the whistling wind as we feel our way through the house, relying on touch and instinct to find our way. My eyes adjust to the absence of light, and I make out shapes and use my wolf senses to find my way. Despite my instincts, the whole black-out thing combined with this howling hurricane gives me the heebie-jeebies. Every slosh of water against the walls outside, every creak in the floor, each exhalation has me jumpy.

"The room's over here," Borris says from somewhere to my right.

"Let's get her out of there," Axel says.

"Honey?" Borris calls through the door. "I brought help."

"Hurry!" his wife yells. "I'm scared. We're sitting on top of the dining room table."

The baby's screams grow louder.

"You think if we work together, we can push the credenza out of the way?" Axel says to Warrick.

"Piece of cake," Warrick says, cracking his knuckles. "Callan and Ethan, you go low. Axel and I will go high. Let's move this motherfucker." He stands before the door, places his palms flat, and widens his legs. Axel stands next to him, matching his position.

Callan and Ethan position their shoulders against the door, crouched between Axel's and Warrick's spread legs. Water has begun seeping across the floor, leaking from under the dining room door as well as the front door.

"On three," booms Axel. "One, two, *three*."

They grunt, straining against the door as it gives a couple of inches.

Small waves slosh against Ethan's and Callan's knees on the floor.

"On, three," Axel commands again. "One, two, *three.*"

They get a few more inches of space in the door.

"One more shot, and we got it," he says. "Ready?"

The other men nod.

"One, two, *three*," he roars, as if priming himself for the ultimate exertion.

This time the door opens wide.

Warrick, Axel, Ethan, and Callan move away from the door. Water rushes out, since apparently the dining room is more flooded. Water drips from Callan and Ethan as they stand. The drips echo into the water sloshing up to their ankles.

Borris rushes into the room as much as one can run while splashing through water in the dark. I can only hear their happy reunion.

"Get the rowboat ready, Luna," Axel says. "We've got to get the woman and baby to safety."

I feel my way through the wet house and make my way out to the porch, where I untie our waiting vessel, proud that they gave me a useful job this time. The men emerge from the house, bumping and feeling for me to make sure I haven't washed away. The water on the porch is at least a foot high now.

"Are you okay, Luna?" Warrick says.

"Fine, fine." I repeat the words, but I'm anything but confident. Every hair on my body is standing at attention.

The woman and her baby clamber out the front door, ushered by Borris.

They climb into the boat.

"Luna's wading with us," Warrick says, wrapping a thick arm around me and pulling me close.

"Luna?" Axel says, checking on me as he takes the rope from my hand. "Everyone ready?"

"Where are we going?" I ask.

"Mischka's mamas. She's got a two-story. We'll all wait on the top floor if we have to," Borris says.

"Let's go, then," Axel says.

We guide the rowboat a couple of blocks down the street as the wind screams and rain tears at us. We have to rely entirely on sound to guide us. The squeals and scrapes of heavy metal alert us to vehicles being pushed in our way. Objects fall with thuds and waves. Things whistle past my head, but I keep my thick hood up, as Axel instructed.

I wonder if the little shack I built in the swamp has been washed away yet, and I get a lonesome feeling in my heart. By the time we arrive at our destination, my senses are on overload. Borris helps his wife and baby from the boat, offers his gratitude, and guides his family into Mischka's mama's home. When they're swallowed up into the house, we turn to go.

"Back in the boat you go, Luna," Warrick says.

"I'm not a baby. I've been taking care of myself my entire life," I protest, but firm hands land around my waist.

"You're my baby girl, and I'm not letting anything happen to you," he says firmly.

"Just get in," Callan says, sounding anxious.

"Hold the boat steady," Warrick says as he hefts me over the lip and places me securely on the seat.

Maybe he can sense the unease, too.

We slosh along in this surreal wildness of nature that beats at us like it longs for our destruction along with its own. It's too much work to yell over the noise of the weather tempest, so we don't try.

Something's about to go wrong—I can feel it in my bones. The storm is moving toward a real hurricane at any moment.

"Callan! Ethan!" I yell.

"What?" they call back in unison.

"Just checking." I wait for a pause and then call, "Axel!"

"Present and accounted for," Axel calls back.

"Good!" I yell as the wind howls. "Warrick?"

"Quit worrying, baby girl. We're all tough guys," he says. "We're all hanging onto the boat."

I can't seem to stop my heart from trying to escape from my chest, though. The storm does its best to splash water into my little vessel.

"The boat's fixing to sink," I yell.

"Shit," someone calls, but I can't tell who it is.

Again, hands grope for my waist and heft me out of the boat. Now we're all forcing our way through the storm, heads down, fighting against the spray and the surge, hoping we don't get hit with any flying debris.

"We're here," Axel calls.

I stop on what feels like the sidewalk, huddling together with the triplets. Axel opens his truck, and the tiny overhead light makes a weak attempt at offering us some light. He grabs flashlights from the cab of his vehicle. "I've got a couple lights I keep in here for emergency breakdowns."

He hands one to Warrick, one to me, and keeps one for himself. He shines his beam at his house, scanning over the roof that's wobbling in the wind. "Shit," he says. "My house isn't going to be spared this time."

The water level at his house is almost to the top step of his porch.

"Let's head over to my place," I call. "My house is on higher ground."

"I've got to grab a few things from inside," Axel says. "I won't be too long. Get yourselves and Luna dry before we all drown in this deluge."

"No way, man," Ethan says. "We're gonna help. Stop being a heroic prick."

"I just got to secure the place," Axel calls. "I'll be out to help in a few minutes." He plods his way up the porch steps, lit by the struggling beam of the flashlight.

"Need help?" I call, weirdly desperate to be near him.

"Stay with them," Axel yells back. "You'll be safer out here!"

A sudden vicious gust of wind blasts through the street, and we all throw our arms up to protect our heads. A loud bang and a clatter compete with the wind's screams.

"What happened?" I cry, training my feeble beam at Axel's house. The roof's now missing, carried away by the hurricane, probably halfway across town by now.

"Oh, no," I cry, staggering through the water toward the house, desperation filling my body "Axel's in there!"

Callan grabs my shoulders, yanking me backwards. "Luna, no! Look out!"

We both stumble against the other two as another blast of wicked wind nearly flattens us. We cling together, but the next second, I hear a loud roar, like a crashing wave but ten times bigger. I whip back around, only to see nothing but a pile of rubble where Axel's beautiful house stood. His home has been utterly destroyed—with him inside.

*

Thank you for reading! Read the thrilling conclusion to his naughty, exciting story here: http://books2read.com/rejectedmate3

To get updates on book 3, sneak peaks and insider info, cover reveals and more, join my B-Team Newsletter: https://www.subscribepage.com/rejected-mate .